DEATH OF A TRAVEL ADVISOR

DORI SALTZMAN

*To all the travel advisors out there whose hard work
and dedication to their craft often goes overlooked and
under-appreciated. I see you.*

$$1$$

"WHAT A WASTE of a perfectly good bottle of champagne," Sophia sighed, adjusting the anchor-print scarf she'd tied around her neck.

"Yes, I know. You've said that already. Now, do you think you can hurry it up a bit? We're supposed to be poolside in less than twenty minutes, or even sooner, if you want to be able to see anything." Tugging on a strand of her black hair, Gabi tried to rein in her impatience with her best friend. Sophia had recently joined her at Best in Travel and was still learning the ropes.

"But why do they have to break the bottle? Wouldn't it be so much better to drink it?" Sophia asked.

"It's good luck. I promise you, I've never gone thirsty at any of the ship christenings I've been to. And you know how much I like my bubbly."

"I know how much you like it mixed with peach juice."

"Who doesn't love a good bellini? Now, can we speed it up, please," Gabi said.

"You're sure you don't want to try calling your aunt one

last time?" Sophia asked, still fiddling with the scarf and glancing at Gabi in the mirror.

Gabi's eyebrows drew together briefly. "If I haven't heard from Aunt Maggie about her biopsy by now, then I'm not going to hear anything today. Even if the doctor calls, she knows the christening starts at four. She won't want to bother me."

Gabi paused, her gaze unfocused, then with a deep breath, she brought herself back into the here and now.

"Now come on. I want to be close enough to see Kristin Bell with my own eyes and not only on the big screen," she said.

"Okay, okay. Let me do my mascara, and then I'll be ready to go. In the meantime, tell me the names of some of the people we'll be meeting up with on the cruise."

"Seriously?" Gabi asked, exasperated with her friend. "I already gave them to you. If you can't remember names, you're never going to make it as a travel advisor."

"It's not that I can't remember names. It's more like, I wasn't really listening when you were talking in the Lyft over here."

"No, you weren't, were you? You were way more interested in our hunky Costa Rican driver."

"Hunky? What is this, 1975? Now, come on. I'm halfway done, and you haven't given me any names yet."

Gabi looked upwards and gave her friend a long give-me-strength huff. Sophia was Gabi's closest friend, but their sense of what constituted as being "on time" differed widely. Gabi was of the *if you're on time, you're late* variety, while Sophia believed showing up on time was an insult to your host.

"The most important person for you to get to know will be Jill. She's our Business Development Manager at

SeaCirque Cruise Line. She's basically your main contact there, and she's a real sweetheart. You'll love her."

"Okay. Jill, BDM, check. Who else?"

"Well, there's Major," Gabi started to say.

"Ooh, that's right. That older advisor you met on the Jamaica familiarization trip last year. I can't wait to meet him!"

"Don't forget that it's fam. No one says familiarization," Gabi reminded Sophia. "You'll also most likely get to meet Stefan Davidson. He's the Senior VP of Sales for SeaCirque."

"Oh, he's that silver fox with the gorgeous blue eyes, right? The one from the Q&A in last week's *Travel Trade Today*?"

Gabi stared at her friend for a moment, her mouth slightly agape. "That's what you remember? That he's a 'silver fox'? You kill me, you know."

Sophia winked a freshly mascaraed eye at Gabi in the mirror. "Okay, all done."

Gabi slipped on her sparkly silver ballet flats, grabbed her silver-flecked purple wrap and sequin-covered clutch, and opened their cabin door. With clutch in hand, she swept her arm in front of her body to indicate to Sophia that she should move.

"I still can't believe that SeaCirque actually got Kristin Bell to agree to be the godmother of *Sea Fantasy*," Sophia gushed, switching gears as she exited the room. "You think we'll get to meet her? That would be amazing."

"That *would* be amazing, but the chances are pretty much slim to none. You know what would also be amazing? If this elevator ever showed up." Gabi pushed the up button for the third time.

"I don't think that helps," Sophia said, gesturing to the button as Gabi pushed it twice more in quick succession.

Gabi made a face at Sophia then pointedly glanced at Sophia's four-inch stilettos. "Why don't we take the stairs?"

"L-O-L," Sophia said dryly. "Oh look, saved by the elevator."

With only four other people on the elevator, there was plenty of room for Gabi and Sophia. The button for Deck 15 was already pressed. Gabi quickly checked her clutch to make sure she had the red invite that would permit them access to the pool deck to watch the naming in person. Others on the cruise would have to watch the proceedings on the big screen in the main theater or on smaller screens in one or two of the larger lounges.

The elevator stopped briefly at Deck 11, where two older ladies with green invites got out, and then it went straight to Deck 15. Exiting the elevator, Gabi and Sophia made their way to the automatic doors on their left, and after showing their invite to two security guards manning the door, they stepped out into a cacophony of loud chatter, laughter, and dance music.

"C'mon. Let's go see if we can find a good spot to stand," Gabi said and grabbed Sophia's hand, pulling her toward the stage.

In front of the stage was the ship's half-Olympic-sized pool, over which lay a bright-blue tarp covered in a thick layer of green, purple, and silver balloons. Waiters carried trays of champagne, and Gabi grabbed two as they squeezed themselves into an open spot near enough to the stage to see clearly.

"Is one of those for me?" Sophia asked, practically having to shout over the noise. "Or are you double fisting it tonight?"

"Ha-ha. Just for that, I should keep both for myself," Gabi said, but she handed one of the flutes over.

Rather than continue to yell over the noise, both women

fell silent, watching the crowd build up around them. Gabi recognized a handful of other travel advisors, as well as a few SeaCirque executives and some members of the travel media. She waved at Debbie, a journalist at a travel trade magazine that she regularly exchanged e-mails with.

As she sipped on her champagne, she felt her clutch vibrate. She contemplated ignoring the text but lasted less than a minute. Knowing that Aunt Maggie, with whom she had lived since she was 13, would not bother her while she was on a work trip, she couldn't help wondering who had sent the text. Gabi's circle of friends was pretty small, and they all knew she was away. She'd left her business cell in the cabin, so it couldn't be a client. She quickly downed the rest of her champagne and waved a waiter with an empty tray over then fished her cell out.

It's bad was all her sister had written. Gabi stared at the message, the words bouncing around in her mind until she felt a hand squeeze her shoulder. She realized Sophia had read the message from behind her.

"I'm so sorry, Gabs."

Gabi tried to focus on her friend's face. The sound of laughter behind her startled her, and she blinked rapidly as the present came rushing back. "What the eff, Alina," Gabi muttered under her breath, but before she could type an angry reply demanding more info, someone squealed behind her.

"There's Kristen Bell!"

Gabi looked to the stage, where the actress was making her way to the microphone. She glanced down at her phone and then back up to the stage. She shoved the phone back into her clutch.

"You okay?" Sophia asked.

"I really don't know," Gabi said. "But what can I do about it now?"

Sophia half smiled and squeezed Gabi's shoulder again. "You can check out the gorgeous Beverly Dream dress Kristin Bell is wearing! What I'd give to have one of her dresses."

Gabi couldn't help but smile. Without thinking, she fished her phone back out to snap a picture of the actress as she raised her hands to hush the crowd.

The next thirty minutes passed as local city and port officials talked about the importance of the *Sea Fantasy* to the fiscal health of Miami and cruise executives gushed over the ship's amenities. Then, a rabbi and priest blessed the ship and all its future passengers.

Finally, the actress hit the button that released the bottle of Dom Perignon. Gabi and Sophia, along with everyone else, watched on the big screen as the bottle of champagne arced through the air. Everyone collectively held their breath until the bottle hit the ship's bow and exploded.

The crowd roared in approval.

"To the *Sea Fantasy*," the women yelled in unison. They raised newly filled flutes as fireworks exploded and confetti rained down on them.

"Has a bottle ever not broken?" Sophia asked.

"Sure, it's happened on occasion. The most infamous is *Costa Concordia*. The bottle didn't break, and less than ten years later, it hit that rock and all those people died."

"Oh wow. Thank goodness it broke here. I don't want to be on a doomed voyage."

Gabi shivered as a cloud settled over the sun. Unfurling her wrap, she threw it around her shoulders. A quick wind had started up; it looked like the perfect weather they'd been having since they arrived in Miami the previous night was starting to turn.

Revelers moved towards the doors to head inside, where the party could continue, rain or shine. Gabi and Sophia joined the crowd, but talk of the Concordia's demise had taken her to a darker place, bringing back thoughts of her aunt. She wasn't sure she was in the mood for the requisite jovial mingling.

"Gabs, you okay?"

"Huh? I guess so. Suddenly not in the mood for lots of schmoozing."

"Well, you better turn that frown upside down because this is my first cruise ship christening, and I'm not letting you drag me down," Sophia said, but her attempt at humor missed the mark and the two fell silent again.

Gabi knew Sophia was right. They were only two of 600 travel advisors invited to attend the *Sea Fantasy*'s inaugural ceremony and the four-day fam cruise afterwards. The rest of the passengers were journalists, company big wigs and partners, and the line's most valued repeat cruisers. It was an honor, and she knew it. As they shuffled their way toward the door, Gabi pushed away thoughts of the text from her sister. She was going to have fun, even if she had to force it.

Absently twirling a strand of her jet-black hair, Gabi took in the scene around her. Though late June, the changing weather had added a chill to the air. She wasn't the only woman hugging a pashmina to herself.

Revelers were still tossing silver, purple, and green confetti around. Others picked bits and pieces of it out of their hair.

The glossy teak deck was littered with the stuff, and the balloon-covered tarp also boasted at least half an inch of it. Gabi felt bad for the deck crew who would have to clean up the mess later on. She hoped for their sake that the rain held off.

"I hope that dour look on your face isn't a reflection of what you think of the *Fantasy*," a voice behind Gabi said.

She immediately recognized the speaker and pushed her glum thoughts aside. "Jill!" She hugged the brunette, genuine warmth tinging her voice. As she stepped back from the hug, she noticed her formerly lanky business development manager's condition for the first time.

"Oh my God, Jill, look at you. You're huge. Why didn't you tell me?"

Jill shrugged. "I don't know. My husband says I'm superstitious, but I find myself reluctant to start the conversation about it. For the most part, I let people figure it out for themselves, which at this point isn't hard to do."

"Well, congratulations. We're thrilled for you." Sophia nudged Gabi aside and hugged Jill as well. "I'm Sophia. It's so nice to meet you."

As always, Gabi had to smile at her best friend's ability to turn any stranger into an immediate fast friend.

"So, what do you think of her?" Jill waved her hand to indicate the ship.

"Oh Jill, she's gorgeous," Gabi said.

"*C'est magnifique!*" Sophia squealed at the same time.

"We haven't seen too much yet," Gabi added, "but what we've seen so far is stunning. I love the wading pool with the water beds. What a cool idea."

"And I'm absolutely in love with the Beverly Dream fashion displays in the atrium," Sophia said.

"Glad you noticed them," said Jill. "She created those outfits exclusively for this ship."

"Ooh, I wish I had the money to buy a Dream original. What do you think, Gabs? Do you think Elaine would mind if I showed up to work in a Dream gown?"

Gabi smiled and shook her head, ignoring Sophia's question. They both knew their boss wouldn't mind at all. Elaine Sinclair was a lovely odd bird and delighted in other peoples' eccentricities. She'd opened Best in Travel when she was 64 years old, after her third husband passed away, leaving her a tidy nest egg. Twenty years later, at a time when most travel advisors worked from home, she insisted on maintaining a storefront and came to work two days a week. She left most of the day-to-day management to Gabi and Lewis, a co-worker who'd joined the company a year after Gabi had, which was now nearly 11 years ago.

"There's so much more for you to see. You'll see it all on your tour tomorrow. And, of course, you've got the next four days to try everything out for yourself," Jill said.

"We can't wait, especially for the spa," Sophia admitted.

"We went straight to the spa to get our massage appointments set in stone when we first got on," Gabi said. "Oh look, there are the Mitchells." She pointed to a couple heading through the doors several people in front of them. "They look like they're having a good time. Remind me later, Jill, to try to introduce you to them. They really appreciated the strings you pulled to get them in one of the Grand Mariner suites."

"I was happy to do it. I know they're your best SeaCirque clients, which makes them some of our best customers too."

"Jill, is your husband here with you?" Sophia asked.

Jill shook her head. "No, I'm flying solo. Well, sort of, anyway," she laughed, placing her hand on her bulging stomach.

"I guess you'll be going on maternity leave?" The thought suddenly occurred to Gabi. "Who's going to handle your accounts while you're gone?"

"We're still figuring it out, but basically, my accounts will be split up among the other reps for the four months that I'm planning to be out. Don't worry. I promise you'll be well taken care of. In fact, your new rep is on the ship, and I'll make sure you meet each other."

"Yeah, okay." Gabi sighed. "I mean, don't get me wrong, Jill. I'm thrilled for you. But I'm definitely going to be sad to see you go. I mean, who's going to guarantee that my clients get the best of everything?" she added half-jokingly.

"Aw, thanks. But I promise I'm not going away forever. Four months'll go by so fast, and then I'll be back. I promise. I love working for SeaCirque. I have no intention of giving it up."

"She'll be back," Sophia said, imitating Arnold Schwarzenegger's famous *Terminator* line, sending all three women into a fit of giggles.

A deep voice cut in on their laughter. "You ladies seem to be having a good time."

"Stefan." Jill smiled up at her boss, who was towering over them. "Hi! We are definitely enjoying the party. Stefan, you remember Gabriella Feraru from Best in Travel, which we inducted into the Ringmaster Club a couple of months ago. And this is Sophia Viscardi. She's new at Best in Travel."

"Hello, Mr. Davidson," Gabi said, offering her hand. She marveled at how attractive he was, just as she had the first time she'd met the man who managed all of SeaCirque's sales. His hair was a beautiful silver, and it was obvious he kept himself fit. But it was his glacial blue eyes that grabbed her attention every time.

At the moment, his distractingly blue eyes were scanning the crowds, as if, Gabi thought, he was looking for someone in particular. But at her greeting, he looked back down at her.

"Stefan, please," he said, taking Gabi's hand in both of his. "It's a pleasure to see you again. I love telling other advisors your success story. It's a great lesson in always being prepared to sell. I myself am always ready to make a deal. There's no one better at it than me." He winked at Jill before looking back at Gabi, his hands still cupping hers.

Gabi's flush deepened now that his attention was fully on her. He was referring to her chance encounter at her dentist's office with a man who arranged events for the National Doctors Under 40 Association. When all was said and done, she'd ended up booking a group of 250 cabins on one of SeaCirque's biggest ships. It's what had gotten them inducted into the Ringmaster Club for top-selling agencies, and it had brought Stefan and Jill up to New Jersey for a personal visit.

"I'm Sophia. It's wonderful to meet you. I read the profile of you in last month's *Travel Trade Today*. It's amazing what you've been able to accomplish at the company," Sophia said, using her hip to gently nudge Gabi aside.

"The pleasure is all mine," Stefan responded. "Welcome to—"

The sound of breaking glass, followed quickly by more breaking glass, interrupted whatever he had been planning to say. Everyone turned to see where the noise had come from. Gabi thought she heard Stefan growl under his breath, but the sound of loud, drunken laughter followed the breaking glass so quickly, she couldn't be sure.

Scant feet away, a thickset man, perhaps in his late 50s, in a Miami Vice-era sky blue sports jacket and tan linen pants was attempting to juggle several champagne flutes. Most had already broken, and he laughed each time another flute exploded upon hitting the wooden deck.

Watching the broken glass shards bounce off the deck, Gabi backstepped, pulling Sophia and Jill with her. *Someone's going to get hurt,* she thought. A second later, she was glad she'd moved, because a piece of glass flew past the spot where they'd been standing.

In the same moment, a tall redhead in a calf-length, rose-patterned sundress grabbed the juggler's arm. The sole remaining airborne flute crashed to the deck.

With one hand still clutching the man's arm, the woman attempted to pry the two glasses the man still held from his pudgy hands, her voice getting louder and louder as he refused to hand them over. Gabi tried to understand what the woman was saying but could only make out a few words through her Irish accent, which her anger had thickened. *Drunk, bully, penniless.* The man clearly did understand and was not pleased. He flicked the woman's hand off his arm with enough force to make her stumble backwards.

"Damn it, Connor," Stefan whispered beside her.

Before he could step forward to intervene, another man stepped out of the crowd. He was red-haired like the woman, although his hair was more rust than fire. But what Gabi noticed most was how powerfully built he was. Taller than the first man, and perhaps a little younger, he was sheer brawn.

The man's voice broke through the loud music and silent crowd. "Aye, watch how you touch my sister."

"Don't you touch me," the first man roared at the woman before turning to the redheaded man. "And you, Brendan, mind your own fucking business." His second warning issued, he turned and rammed himself through the watching crowd.

"Watchin' out for my sister is my business," the man called Brendan yelled at his back. "And I'll kill you if you ever shove her like that again."

Looking startled then embarrassed when she realized everyone was staring, the woman quickly turned and left in the opposite direction, her brother following swiftly after her.

2

———

"I HONESTLY CAN'T BELIEVE that guy is a travel agent."

Gabi and Sophia were still discussing the juggling incident the next morning as they rode the elevator up to Deck 11.

"And not just any travel *advisor*," Gabi emphasized the word to remind her best friend they didn't use the five-letter "a" word. The word "agent," she'd told her friend many times, doesn't encompass everything advisors do for their clients. Plus, it implies they work for the suppliers they're selling, not the people who come to them for help. "He must be a top-selling advisor, or he wouldn't have been invited on this sailing."

"I don't get it. Who'd want to work with a guy like that? I wouldn't want to exchange two sentences with that man, let alone have him plan my vacation."

"Maybe Jill's right. Maybe he does bully clients into booking with him," Gabi said, remembering what Jill had sarcastically said the previous night.

"Maybe he could land a first-time client, but after that? Who would stay with him?"

"I don't know." The elevator door opened, and they stepped out. The entrance to the ship's buffet feet away. "Our ship tour starts in 25 minutes. Let's grab something and take it down with us."

"Aw, Gabs, I'd rather grab a quick bite here than try to balance food with taking photos and notes," Sophia pleaded.

"Eat fast, then. I don't want to be late."

Thirty minutes later, the two friends joined a group of about twenty others milling around the atrium and chatting.

"See, we're not late," Sophia said, grabbing a mimosa off a tray a waiter was carrying through the group. "You worry too much."

"And you dawdle too much."

"Well, I couldn't resist chatting with John Clarke. It was nice of Jill to find us in the buffet to bring him over for an introduction. He seems like he'll do a good job while Jill is out on maternity. Plus, I love his Irish brogue. So sexy."

"Anyone with a Y chromosome is sexy to you, Soph," Gabi retorted, but secretly she agreed. His accent and the adorable dimples he sported when he smiled–which seemed to be always–definitely made their new BDM attractive.

"Don't be jealous." Sophia laughed. "Just because you've made the choice to not go out on a date in like ten years doesn't mean the rest of us have to forego the pleasure of the opposite sex."

"Hey, I've been on dates. Or are you forgetting the ever-rotating roster of blind dates that you and BJ are always bringing around to pub trivia? Besides, isn't John a teeny bit too old for you?" Sophia stuck her tongue out at Gabi, then wandered off to check out the Beverly Dream fashion display. Gabi strolled after her, checking out the atrium while she walked.

In keeping with the fantastical motif of the ship, the Dream Atrium was designed to evoke the surreal quality of a dreamscape. The carpeting was a swirl of psychedelic purples, pinks, silvers, and greens. The atrium's centerpiece was a stunning clear crystal column, which rose from Deck 4 to 5. Inside the crystal, holographic butterflies in a riot of colors appeared to flit about. A translucent marble staircase spiraled around the column.

As she marveled at the decor, Gabi spotted Jill on the other side of the atrium. She had been cornered by two older women, each one with a hand placed on her stomach. She looked like she needed rescuing.

"Excuse me, sorry." Gabi shouldered her way between the two women. "Jill, may I speak with you? In private?"

"Yes, of course. Please excuse us," Jill said, and the women stepped away. "Thanks Gabi," Jill said as soon as the women were out of earshot.

"Gabi! Is that you, darlin'?"

Gabi turned to the speaker, a smile spreading across her face. "Major!" she exclaimed and stepped forward into a warm hug. She hadn't seen her friend since the previous year. She, along with her sister Alina, had bonded with the older advisor during hours' long, and usually tedious, property inspections on a Jamaica fam trip the year before. It had been the first time since her dad died when she was 12 that she and her sister had spent extended time together, and Major had helped them through their rougher moments. Since then, Gabi and Major had talked on the phone and e-mailed back and forth. He looked much the same as the last time she'd seen him, with his silver hair cropped short and his khaki shorts and ivory button-up shirt immaculately pressed.

"How's your aunt doing?" he asked. She'd told him earlier in the week about Aunt Maggie's biopsy.

"Not great, but let's save that conversation for another time. The last thing I need is to get all emotional now."

Major squeezed her hand briefly then turned to greet Jill.

"Major," Jill said, kissing him on the cheek. "I didn't think you were coming."

"What, and miss a chance to see my favorite sales gal *and* my favorite fellow travel agent? Not a chance." Inwardly, Gabi cringed at Major's use of the word agent, but she knew it was futile to try to get him to call himself an advisor. He'd grown up in the era of travel agents, so a travel agent he was.

"Well, I'm so glad you decided to join us, despite everything."

Gabi cocked her head at Jill, then Major, unclear what Jill meant when she'd said "everything." For a moment, she detected a slight droop to Major's normally ramrod straight posture, but then he smiled and threw one arm over her shoulders and his back was straight as ever.

"Now, don't you be worryin' about that, darlin'. You got plenty to keep you busy, what with being ready to foal and all."

Gabi and Jill laughed at his choice of words. Major had almost forty years in the military, but he was still a country boy at heart.

"You must be Major," Sophia said, stepping up to Gabi's side. "I've heard so much about you. I'm Sophia."

"Mighty pleased to meet you, ma'am," Major said, offering her his hand.

Sophia ignored the outstretched hand. "I feel like I already know you from everything Gabi's said about you. Is it okay if I give you a hug?"

"Ma'am, I'd be honored," Major said and opened his arms. "It's such a pleasure to be in such charming company. Used to be that most of the gals on these trips were usually, ah—" he paused and cleared his throat intentionally "—um, a shade closer in age to myself." He winked at the women and smiled.

"So, Major? Is that a nickname or an actual rank?" Sophia asked.

"Both, actually. Major George Thomas at your service. Served in the US Air Force for thirty-seven years, but I've been out of that game for almost ten years now. But the name Major stuck. Only my wife calls me George anymore."

"Speaking of your wife. She wouldn't by any chance happen to be a pretty, dark-haired woman wearing a lavender dress," Gabi asked.

Major turned to follow her gaze. A woman Gabi estimated to be in her mid-sixties was waving at him.

"That'd be the missus. She gets jealous if I spend too long with beautiful young women," he joked.

"Well then, Major, you'd better go. Clearly, you don't want to keep your general waiting," Gabi joked back.

Major threw his head back and laughed, offered the three women a small salute, and headed toward his wife.

"He's wonderful," cooed Sophia.

"He really is," Jill agreed. "He bought a Cruising Away franchise about eight years ago and quickly became one of our best partners."

Her smile faded. "But he's had some issues over the past few years. He had a heart attack about three years ago and ended up taking a break from work for a few months."

"Wow, he never said," Gabi replied. "We met last year, and he seemed fit as a fiddle. Never once showed any signs of having a bad heart. And in the months since, he's never said anything to me about it."

Jill lowered her voice. "Did he say anything to you about losing business to someone else? Someone he accused of stealing his clients?"

"No! Nothing. We've been e-mailing back and forth for months, and he never mentioned anything. Major doesn't seem like the kind of guy who'd go around idly making accusations like that. Was there any truth to his claims?" Gabi asked. Stealing another advisor's clients was about the worst sin a travel advisor could commit.

"The company looked into it, but we couldn't find any evidence of wrongdoing. There was nothing to indicate that the clients who left Major didn't simply decide to switch to another advisor of their own accord. Especially since he'd taken a break and was having another advisor handle his clients for him while he was out. Maybe that person didn't offer the service his clients had gotten used to with Major."

"Did he lose a lot of business?" Gabi asked.

"About half the groups he usually booked in a year."

"Ouch, that's a lot," Sophia said. "Poor guy."

As Sophia asked Jill more about what could be done to help Major, a woman in a ship officer's uniform holding a clipboard approached the milling group of travel advisors.

"Damn," Gabi swore, interrupting their conversation. "I've got to pee. If they start the tour before I get back, do me a favor and take notes on anything that seems important. Thanks." Gabi shoved a notebook and pen into Sophia's free hand and darted down the nearest corridor.

The path led through the ship's fine jewelry shopping area. Gabi hurried past, barely noticing the displays of pricey gold and precious gems as she sidestepped shoppers browsing items that were well out of her budget.

Exiting the shopping area, she frowned when she saw the men's bathroom. Having been on many cruise ships before, she quickly calculated that the ladies' room would be in the corridor running parallel to where she was, on the other side of the ship. Ahead was a short passageway that would take her from the port to starboard side, but as she approached, she heard a man yelling loudly. Hesitant to barge into someone's fight, but also more than a little bit curious, she stopped and peeked around the corner.

She was just in time to see a man shove someone backwards, past the opposite corner, but she couldn't see the person who had been shoved.

"Don't you dare threaten me," the shover yelled.

Gabi recognized him as the champagne flute juggler of the night before. Connor, the redheaded Irish woman had called him. He, however, was not at all Irish. His accent was pure New York City. Brooklyn, Gabi guessed.

He was dressed in the same outfit as the previous night, except the shirt he wore under the light-blue sports jacket was now a garish yellow. His beefy face was red and blotchy.

"Don't you dare get all high and mighty with me," he continued yelling. "You always thought you was better than me, but you ain't any different. You wouldn't be nowhere without me." He paused for a moment, perhaps to listen to the other person's reply, and then spoke again. "This ends when I say it ends, you got that?"

Gabi saw him shove at the other person again and then turn around and head toward the corridor she was occupying. She pulled back and turned toward the shops so he wouldn't notice her as he stormed past her in the direction of the atrium.

Her curiosity fully aroused, Gabi quickly darted around the corner and toward the starboard side corridor. She listened for any sound to indicate that the other person was still there. When she didn't hear anything, she carefully stepped into the hallway. The door to the ladies' room was in front of her, and the hallway was completely empty, all the way down toward the atrium.

Perhaps Connor had been arguing with a woman, Gabi thought. But the ladies' room was as empty as the corridor.

Could he have shoved a woman? Gabi wondered as she washed her hands a few minutes later. *Would he?* She thought about the redhead in the rose-patterned dress the night before and remembered the look of pure rage on the man's face. *Yep, he wouldn't hesitate,* she concluded.

Knowing it was futile to dwell on the matter further, Gabi jogged back to the atrium. She arrived right as her tour group was exiting the other side. Catching up, she retrieved her notebook and pen from Sophia. Written in Sophia's chicken scratch handwriting was a line of notes: *4,200 people, 12 decks, 23 cabin categories.*

"We're now passing two of our main specialty dining venues," said their tour guide, a bubbly young woman who was clearly one of the kids' club staffers. "This is Butler's, our steakhouse, and over here is Ciao Bella. Their risottos are to die for."

The next two hours were spent touring the ship's public spaces, as well as viewing several of the stateroom categories, including the higher-priced suites.

As they were passing through the last of the public spaces, after having exited the 800-person main theater onboard, Sophia nudged Gabi. "There's John Clarke again," she said, pointing to the ship's small card room, where their new Business Development Manager was engaged in what seemed to be an animated argument with a man whose back was to them. Sophia waved when John noticed them passing. He winked back at her.

"That's weird," Gabi said, craning her neck to take one last look at the two men.

"What is?" Sophia asked.

"The guy John was arguing with back there. I'm pretty sure that's the big guy who got into it with the champagne juggler last night."

"How could you tell? His back was to us."

"I know, but I doubt there are too many men onboard with his build *and* that color hair. I wonder how they know each other."

"Don't most of the advisors and BDMs know each other?"

"Maybe, but enough to be arguing that heatedly? Plus, I'm not sure that guy's an advisor."

"*Ahem.*" Their tour guide cleared her voice and stared pointedly at Gabi and Sophia.

Sorry, Gabi mouthed, returning to taking notes as the woman continued with her description of the various entertainment venues on the *Sea Fantasy*.

Following the tour, Gabi's small group of travel advisors joined about 100 others in Mirage, a lounge that doubled as a secondary theater and meeting space.

As they settled into their seats, Gabi felt her phone buzz in her sweater pocket. Hoping it might be a response from either her aunt or her sister, she took it out to glance at. It was a WhatsApp message from a friend confirming she and Sophia would be around for pub trivia night in two weeks' time. Gabi quickly typed a response then put her phone away.

"Was that your sister?" Sophia asked.

"No, it was BJ. Apparently, Alina doesn't think it's important enough to get back to me. I expect that from Aunt Maggie during a work trip, but not Alina. Not after sending that super informative text last night!"

"It's only 10:30. Maybe she hasn't found time yet. I'm sure your nephews are keeping her busy on a Saturday morning."

"Too busy to explain a cryptic text like that? How bad is bad? Like 'beyond help' bad? Or 'it's going to be a fight but she can make it' bad?"

"Is this seat taken?"

Gabi jumped, surprised she hadn't noticed her friend sidle up next to her.

"Major," Sophia smiled at the friendly septuagenarian. "We were hoping you'd show up. We've been saving a seat for you."

Gabi had to laugh at her friend's blatant lie. The row they'd chosen, about midway from the stage, as well as the rows around them were mostly unoccupied, so there were plenty of empty seats and no saving required. Her laugh petered out as her phone vibrated again, and again, it was her friend BJ and not her sister.

"Gabi? You okay, gal?" Major asked.

She glared at her phone, before shoving it back into her pocket.

"You look like you're raring to do someone some damage," he added. "I hope it wasn't anything I said."

"Huh? Oh, no Major, it's not you," Gabi reassured him. "I've been expecting a message from my sister all morning, and so far, nada."

As they spoke, Stefan Davidson made his way on stage, stopping to talk to two women, one of whom handed him a bottle of water. For a brief moment, Major's demeanor hardened and he watched Stefan with narrowed eyes.

"Are you okay, Major?" It was Gabi's turn to ask the question.

"That man," he growled. Then he cleared his throat and looked back to Gabi, his face softening. "Let's just say that man is not one of my favorite people."

"Does that have something to do with the guy who stole your clients?" Sophia asked.

"Sophia!" Gabi rounded on her friend. "I don't think that's any of our business. I'm so sorry, Major. Jill mentioned something this morning."

Major had started at Sophia's question, and for a second,

Gabi recognized real anger in his eyes. But as he looked at Sophia and her, he blinked the emotion away and his usual gentle demeanor returned. He coughed quietly as he snuck another glance at Stefan, who was now standing at the podium, fiddling with some papers. "It's okay," Major said, patting Sophia's hand. "Don't you worry your pretty head about it for one more second."

"Good morning, ladies and gentleman," Stefan said, and the crowd, including Gabi, Sophia, and Major, quieted down. "I hope you enjoyed this morning's tour of *Sea Fantasy*. She's been three years in the making, and we're all very proud of her."

Gabi tucked her right leg under her body as she settled in to listen to Stefan's presentation, much of which repeated what she'd already learned during the tour. An hour and several videos about cabin types, group options, and marketing ideas later, her grumbling stomach began to protest the lengthy talk. Next to her, Sophia was fidgeting restlessly in her seat. The travel advisor in the seat in front of her had long ago stopped taking notes and was instead sketching what appeared to be a cocktail umbrella.

"All right, folks. I can see most of you are ready for a break," Stefan said, finally bringing the presentation to an end. "We have lunch set up for you in the Chimera restaurant. If you don't remember, that's two decks up and toward the front of the ship."

Gabi, Sophia, and Major joined the rest of the hungry travel advisors in gathering up their belongings and making their way toward the theater's exit.

"And please remember," Stefan added. "Parasailing starts at 2:00. Everyone who signed up should have already received their appointed time. Because the entire system is computerized and based on various criteria, it's important that we stick with the schedule as is. If you miss your time slot, you won't get another chance."

Already outside the theater and halfway to the stairs, Major stopped.

"Excuse me, ladies. I just remembered I'm supposed to have a quick word with Stefan. Perhaps you'll save a seat for me at lunch?"

"Of course, Major. See you in a few."

"So, what do you think Major and Stefan are talking about?" Sophia asked Gabi as they stood in line waiting for the buffet. In front of them, a woman in a "For a good time, call a travel advisor" T-shirt complained to the server that the shrimp was almost gone.

"I'd guess that Major wants Stefan to do something about whoever is stealing his clients," Gabi whispered. "But I don't think this is the best place to be talking about it. Too many ears to overhear. Plus, Major didn't want to talk about it before, so we should probably leave it alone. It's none of our business."

"You think Stefan can do anything?" Sophia asked, ignoring Gabi's warning.

"Soph, we can talk about it later. Like when there are fewer people around." Gabi stared hard at her friend, tilting her head towards the people surrounding them.

"Well, I'd be furious if anyone stole one of my clients and the person in charge didn't do anything about it."

"Sophia," Gabi snapped.

Sophia flinched and paused, a ladle of salad dressing in hand. "Don't snap at me, Gabi."

"Then stop talking about it."

The two friends glared at each other.

Gabi broke eye contact first. "Fine, I'm sorry. I shouldn't have snapped. But you shouldn't have kept asking."

"Are you sure that's what's bothering you?" Sophia pressed.

"I don't know. Maybe not. I'm totally wound up right now. I still haven't heard from Alina, and Aunt Maggie hasn't e-mailed me. I have no idea how she's doing. *All* I know is what Alina said in her text. But what did she even mean?" Gabi would have thrown her arms in the air if she hadn't been holding her buffet tray with both hands.

"I know," Sophia said, pressing her lips together in the universal half-smile, half-frown that denoted sympathy. "Hopefully, you'll hear something from at least one of them before we have to head upstairs for the parasailing."

"Hey, the line starts in the back, buddy," a travel advisor yelled at someone who had cut the line to get to the cold cuts.

Gabi was not surprised to see that the line cutter was Connor, the champagne juggler she'd last seen fighting with someone. The man clearly couldn't keep himself out of trouble. She felt her cheeks heat up as she watched him.

"Mind your business, old man," Connor snarled. He loaded his plate with meat then cut the line again to grab a roll.

"Oh no, not today," Gabi muttered as she watched Connor take a seat at the table where she and Sophia had placed their belongings. Three others at the table looked up, startled, when he slammed his tray down.

"Maybe he'll wolf down his food and be gone before we get back to the table," Sophia offered, though they were nearly at the end of the buffet offerings.

"If not, I may have to give him a piece of my mind. The way he treats people is despicable. And that ugly display last night? Somebody needs to say something." All the unease and anxiety she'd been feeling funneled quickly into a white-hot focus on the man who was making everyone around him miserable.

"Gabs," Sophia warned. "Be careful. From what we've seen of this guy, I don't trust him. Let's hope he moves on quickly. And if he doesn't, just ignore him. Gabi?"

"Hmmph" was the only reply Sophia got.

They moved on to a pop-up bar manned by a crewmember to get themselves a drink. It took less than two minutes to order and be served their drinks and get back to their table. Connor was still there.

Just as Gabi and Sophia sat down, a woman in short shorts and a crop top approached Connor.

"Connor, I need to talk to you."

Connor ignored her, scrolling through something on his phone.

"Now," she added.

He slowly put his phone down on the table and looked up at her. "What do you want, Tanya?"

"The same thing I wanted this morning. My money. You owe me—"

"Nothing. I owe you nothing. You keep coming at me with this, and you'll get something. But it won't be money."

"You're threatening me? You? If the cops knew half the things I know…" She left the threat hanging.

"You better watch yourself, Tanya," Connor started to say.

"No. You better watch yourself. You're going to pay up, one way or another. This is your last chance." With that, she turned and walked away.

Connor started to get up from his chair to go after her, but his phone rang. He listened to the speaker for less than a minute before yelling into the phone.

"Don't you dare… No, you're not. This is my deal, and I

don't give a rat's ass what your sister said. You ain't a part of it. And tell that nosy bitch to keep outta my business if she knows what's good for her. You hear me, Brendan?" Connor's voice got louder. "Brendan? Damn it!" He slammed his cell phone down and noticed that everyone at the table was staring at him. "What the hell are you looking at?" he demanded.

"One of the rudest people I've ever encountered in my life," Gabi answered.

"Gabi!" Sophia gasped.

The other three people at the table froze in astonishment then quickly averted their eyes and began shoveling food into their mouths.

Just then, a large hand clamped down on Connor's shoulder. "Ah, Connor, boyo. Causin' trouble yet again, are you? Never were much good at makin' friends." He turned to Gabi and Sophia. "Brendan O'Malley at yer service, ladies."

Gabi blinked up at Brendan. Up close, he was even larger than he'd appeared the night before. She looked from Brendan to Connor. He hadn't lost the predatory look she'd seen in his eyes during his confrontation with the short-shorts woman, but now his attention was focused on Brendan. Gabi realized she was holding her breath and inhaled sharply as the tension between the men spread out beyond them. The woman sitting next to Sophia grabbed the man next to her and fled the table.

Brendan sat in the empty chair next to Connor. Even sitting, he towered over Connor. His hand was still forcefully keeping Connor in his seat. "I apologize for my brother-in-law. He can be a bit prickly at times. Or is that a bit of a prick?" He chuckled at his own joke. "Good thing we're goin' into business together, isn't it? I can keep a better eye on you that way." Brendan's hand moved from Connor's shoulder to slap him on the back.

"Get offa me." Connor swung his arm up, forcing Brendan's hand away from his back. Despite the difference in size, Connor clearly wasn't cowed by Brendan at all. He shoved his chair back and rose. Brendan stood as well.

Whoa, that man is a wall, Gabi thought.

"Gabi, let's go," Sophia whispered, tugging at Gabi's sweater.

But she couldn't tear her attention away from the two men.

"We are not, and never will be, going into business together, Brendan."

Brendan took a half step closer, his whispered words barely carrying to Gabi. "Say it, Connor. Go on. Say, 'over my dead body.' Cause that's what you're gonna be if you're not careful."

Gabi drew back at the barely repressed violence radiating from the two men. She was sure one of the men was going to take a swing at the other. As she finally started to stand to get away from the men, she noticed Major storming towards their table.

"You son of a bitch!" Major bellowed. "I don't care what SeaCirque says. You're not taking any more of my clients."

Brendan was thrown back as Major grabbed Connor by the back of the shirt and spun him around. A right hook caught Connor on the chin, knocking him off balance. He crashed into the table, knocking dishes and glasses everywhere. Gabi and Sophia jumped out of their seats to escape the melee. Connor had landed on a plate of French fries, and as he pushed himself back up, Gabi could see ketchup smeared across his back.

Connor roared, bent over, and prepared to tackle Major NFL-style, but Brendan stepped in between the two men. His sheer size absorbed Connor's momentum. As Brendan was stopping Connor, two security officers appeared and grabbed Major.

"Get off of me," Major yelled.

"Let me at him," Connor yelled.

"You steal another one of my clients and I'll kill you, you hear me?" Major screamed at Connor as security dragged him out of the restaurant.

3

____

GABI CRANED HER NECK, scanning the crowd. She and Sophia were at the back of the ship, standing on the jogging track, which encircled Deck 7 of the *Sea Fantasy*. Above them, on a half-deck, a group of men practiced their golf swings in the small mesh-enclosed driving range.

"Any sign of Major?" Sophia asked.

They hadn't seen the older travel advisor since he'd been hauled off by security. Not that they'd really seen anyone. They, along with several others who'd been in the restaurant at the time of Major's attack on Connor, had been asked to stay and answer some questions. The task had forced Gabi and Sophia to skip their planned pre-parasailing cabin break. They'd only gotten to Deck 7 with enough time to grab a decent spot along the promenade from which to watch as the first few groups got to try out SeaCirque's newest at-sea attraction.

"I don't see him anywhere. Maybe he's still with security," Gabi said. "I can't believe Connor is the one who's been stealing Major's clients. Well, actually, I can believe it, but still. And," she continued, "how many times did security need to ask us the same questions about their fight? Because of them, I'm now behind on responding to yesterday's booking inquiries. I think it was pretty obvious why Major attacked the guy."

Sophia glanced at Gabi sympathetically. "We could skip the parasailing, if you want."

Gabi considered Sophia's suggestion. Since being released by security, she'd had the same thought a couple of times. Between worrying about her aunt and the amount of work she had to make up, skipping out on the parasailing made a lot of sense. But she'd always wanted to try it, and it normally cost too much for her yearly budget to absorb. Plus, Aunt Maggie would kill her if she found out Gabi had missed out because she'd been worrying about her.

"No. I'm already signed up, and I want to see how it all works before I go," Gabi sighed. "It's not like Aunt Maggie has e-mailed me. Or Alina, for that matter."

Sophia not so subtly changed the subject back to Major. "You know, I still can't believe Major attacked Connor like that."

Gabi hooked a few loose strands of hair behind her ear, tightened her ponytail, and smiled gratefully at Sophia. "Well, he was angry. Really angry."

"I guess. You know me though. I don't think violence is ever the answer. I mean, what did punching Connor accomplish? Major's locked up with security while Connor is out here, free as a bird." She pointed to where Connor was gathered with a small cluster of people.

"Violence isn't an answer," Gabi agreed. "But sometimes, you have to stand up to the bullies or else they'll keep walking over you. You of all people should understand that," Gabi said, reminding Sophia how the two of them had met, when Gabi had gotten in between Sophia and two bigger girls who had been picking on her, back when they were fifteen.

"You can't be everyone's hero, Gabs. Sometimes facing off against a bully isn't the best idea. Speaking of bullies, how do you think Connor got to be in the first group to go parasailing?"

They both looked back down to where Connor was waiting at the back of Deck 3. He, along with nine others, were waiting at the top of a stairway leading down to a retractable platform, currently extending out about twenty feet from the back of the ship.

"Good question. Um, is that John Clarke he's talking to?" Gabi asked. The women shared a curious look. "First, we see John talking to Brendan. Later, Brendan gets into it with Connor, and now, John is talking to Connor. Strange company our new BDM is keeping, don't you think?" Gabi pondered aloud.

She and Sophia kept their voices low as they spoke. They were surrounded by onlookers who had come, like them, to watch SeaCirque's latest at-sea attraction. She was among the select few in the crowd who would get a chance to give the parasailing a try later that day. Gabi had earned her spot by qualifying as one of the cruise line's top-selling advisors for the previous year.

As they watched, Connor angrily waved John away, almost pushing him as he did so, and then stepped onto the staircase. John, meanwhile, looked behind himself and shook his head. Gabi followed his line of sight until she spotted the redheaded woman they'd seen the night before. Like Gabi and Sophia, she had found a spot along the promenade. The woman scowled back at John before turning her glare on Connor. Next to her was Brendan. His stare was also fixed solidly on Connor.

Gabi nudged Sophia, using her chin to point Sophia in the direction of Brendan and the woman.

"Ohh. Interesting."

"Look at the way they're glaring at Connor," Gabi said. "Seriously, if looks could kill… I can't believe he doesn't feel it."

Down on the platform, Connor, Stefan Davidson, and several others listened as two men in SeaCirque-branded jumpsuits demonstrated safety rules. When they finished, they gestured for Stefan to step forward and into the parasailing harness. The two men then buckled him up, checking and rechecking everything to make sure he was good to go.

As she watched, Gabi sensed movement behind her and turned her head to look. Major was maneuvering through the people crowded behind her and Sophia. With Major was his wife, the pretty dark-haired woman he'd pointed out to them a couple hours earlier.

"Ah, my two favorite fillies," Major said as he finally reached them. Though he smiled as he said the words, his voice sounded forced and his smile was fleeting.

He looks tired, she thought.

Sophia gave Major a quick one-arm hug. "I'm glad you're okay, Major. We were afraid they had locked you up for the rest of the cruise."

"Nah, they got a call from Stefan to let me go, but I got a stern warning to keep my distance. Thankfully, the little lady showed up to calm me down."

Major wrapped his arm around his wife.

"Not calm enough," she scolded. "I can tell your blood pressure is up. You keep rubbing your chest, and you're too pale. I wanted him to go back to the cabin and rest, but he wouldn't hear of it," she said to Gabi and Sophia.

"That's what the nitroglycerin was for, woman. Stop worryin'. I'll be fine in a few minutes."

She sighed in resignation and introduced herself to Gabi and Sophia. "I'm Violet. George's, er, Major's wife. It's nice to finally meet you, Gabi. And nice to meet you as well, Sophia."

"You know, I always forget your real name isn't Major," Gabi laughed, deciding the best thing to do was ignore the couple's argument. "It's a pleasure to meet you too. Major never stopped talking about you last year." Now that Gabi could see her up close, she realized Violet was younger than she had thought. She must be closer to mid-50s than mid-60s, she guessed.

"You okay now?" Gabi asked Major.

Major's color wasn't quite back to normal, but he wasn't as ashen as a moment ago. He looked down at Stefan and Connor, his eyes narrowed. She could see his grip tightening on Violet's shoulders. In response, Violet gently rubbed circles on the back of his hand.

"I'm fine," Major said, but his voice was too deep, too gravelly. "I'll be better soon enough."

Gabi's brows drew together, startled by the venom in his voice. In spite of the bright sunshine warming her skin, she shivered.

"There he goes," Sophia cried out.

Below them, the wind had gently snagged the green, silver, and purple parasail attached to Stefan. Ever so slowly, he was lifted off the platform and drawn into the air. Higher and higher he floated, until he was merely a large dot in the sky above them.

"He looks nervous," Sophia remarked. "Look how tightly he's holding on to the straps."

"I hope he's scared shitless," Major growled, teeth clenched.

Gabi darted a quick look at Major. His hands were shoved into his pockets, and his normally erect shoulders were hunched together. During the five-day fam trip they'd met on the year before, she'd never once heard him curse. He certainly never cursed in their e-mail correspondence. Connor had definitely gotten under his skin. Violet had her arms around him, and she was whispering to him.

The dot that was Stefan grew larger as he descended, until softly, the wind deposited him back on the platform.

"You don't get to stay up very long, do you?" Sophia asked Gabi.

"I think the description said five minutes. Seems like more than enough to me. I mean, we're in the middle of the sea, so there's not much to see up there," Gabi responded.

Next to her, she felt Major tense up even more. Below, Connor stepped forward as Stefan stepped out of the harness. As Stefan passed Connor, he clapped Connor on the back and leaned in toward Connor's ear.

Gabi glanced to where she'd last seen Connor's wife standing with Brendan. She was still glaring down at him, but Brendan had disappeared. Scanning the crowd, Gabi spied him standing near the staircase that led down to the parasailing platform. Pressed against the railing, he was also staring daggers at Connor.

One of the parasail handlers inspected Connor's buckles, while the second handler double checked the silk parachute. A thumbs-up was given, the parachute released, and Connor rose smoothly into the air.

"I wish we had binoculars. I'd love to see the look on your face when it's your turn and you're all the way up there," Sophia said to Gabi.

Like Stefan before him, Connor was a dark dot in the sky, framed by the colorful sail behind him.

"What the... Why is he waving his arms like that?" Gabi asked no one in particular, squinting to try to see better.

Around her, the crowd began murmuring as Connor's waves seemed to get more frantic.

"I don't remember Stefan hanging like that," Sophia said.

"Like what? I don't see…" Gabi paused. "Oh, yeah, you're right. He's definitely hanging from the parachute kinda lopsided."

"Oh my God!" someone yelled.

Off to Gabi's left, a woman screamed, and people all across the decks gasped as Connor plummeted toward the ocean, separated from the parachute, which still floated gracefully in the air. As he fell, he hit the cable that held the parachute to the ship. His leg snagged on the cable line, and his knee somehow hooked over it, stopping his momentum for a quick second before he continued down until he hit the water.

Stefan ran forward to the edge of the platform at the same time as the ship's emergency horn sounded. Dozens of crewmembers yelled, "Man overboard." Crew who had been watching along with the crowd turned and began pushing them back as a lifeboat was deployed.

"Ladies and gentlemen, the captain has issued an emergency alert. Please follow the nearest crew member to a muster station. This is not a drill," the cruise director's voice blared out of the speakers from directly overhead.

Sophia grabbed Gabi's hand as they were herded away from the railing. Looking over her shoulder, she saw Major resist Violet's attempts to move him. His eyes were locked on the parasail that was slowly floating back down toward the ocean's surface. She couldn't be sure, but it looked like he was smiling.

~

"How much longer are you going to keep us here?" a man demanded of a ship officer standing on the stage.

"Sir, please try to be patient."

"Patient? We've been waiting here for more than two hours already," the man yelled.

"Please, sir, sit down. Let me see if I can get any more information."

Gabi watched as the officer pulled out his ship phone. Gabi glanced at her watch. *Closer to two and a half hours,* she thought.

"This is insane," Sophia commented. "Why are they keeping us here?"

"Because someone died," Major said, pulling his gaze from wherever his mind had been.

Gabi, Violet, and Sophia all looked at Major. It was the first time he'd spoken since they'd been brought to the Neptune Theater along with everyone else who'd been watching the parasailing from the outer decks when the accident happened. Gabi had exchanged several worried looks with Violet over the past two hours as Major had continued to sit without speaking, staring into space, lost in his own thoughts.

"Whether it was an accident or not, the captain has to treat it like a crime scene."

"Meaning the crew is securing the parasailing platform and all the equipment. And rounding up all the witnesses, which is us," Gabi said.

Three surprised faces stared at her in response. "Dad, cop," she reminded them.

"That's exactly right," Major confirmed. "Until the captain feels that everything is totally secure, I doubt they're going to let us go anywhere. And I can guarantee SeaCirque has already contacted the Coast Guard and the FBI."

"I think we're about to find out more," Violet said,

pointing to the officer on stage, who had picked up the microphone.

"Ladies and gentlemen, thank you very much for your patience. We know it's been a long afternoon. We are currently on our way back to Port Canaveral. When we arrive tomorrow morning, FBI agents will be boarding the ship. They have informed us that they will want to speak with anyone who witnessed the incident.

"For now, you will be free to go momentarily. You'll be going row by row, starting with the row in the back. As you leave the theater, a crew member will scan your keycard. You will receive a notice later today to let you know when and where you'll need to be tomorrow. Until then, all regular activity will resume aboard ship. Again, thank you for your understanding and your patience."

The officer turned the microphone off and waved to the security crew at the back of the theater, who quickly got everyone in the back two rows up and headed out of the theater.

"Finally!" Sophia exclaimed. "I don't know about you guys, but I've been needing to pee for the past hour!"

"I'm with you," Violet agreed.

"Well, thankfully, there's only a few more rows until we get to go," Gabi said, watching as row after row of people filed out of the theater, getting their keycard scanned as they exited. "Oh, there are my clients, the Mitchells. I wonder if they're gonna freak out on me later."

"They shouldn't." Sophia said. "It's not like it's your fault Connor got himself killed."

Gabi winced at Sophia's choice of words. The way she said it implied that Connor's death was someone's fault. She was sure it had been a horrible accident. Yet, she couldn't get the image of Brendan towering over Connor, threating him, out of her mind.

"I'd be willing to bet almost every single one of us has at least one client caught up in this mess," Major said, interrupting Gabi's thoughts. "Some of them are going to take their anger out on us, and thankfully, others will be more understanding. Hopefully SeaCirque will step up with some future cruise credits to appease everyone."

Flashes of angry clients displaced the image of Brendan and Connor in Gabi's head, and she groaned. "You think SeaCirque will take all the irate calls for us too?"

Major tapped Gabi's chin with a knuckle. "Chin up, soldier."

"Right, chin up," she sighed.

"We're next," Sophia said, practically hopping from foot to foot. Two minutes later, she shoved her belongings into Gabi's arms and, with Violet in tow, made a beeline for the nearest bathroom.

"Are you okay, Major?" Gabi asked as they waited. "You were pretty quiet in there for a while."

Major stared into space for a moment then gave Gabi a half smile. "I'm fine. I'm just in shock like everyone else. Can't say I'm sorry the guy is gone, but that was…" Major shook his head. He left the sentence unfinished as Violet and Sophia emerged from the bathroom.

For a moment, the four stood in silence as people streamed past them, heading back to their cabins or to the buffet for food.

Violet was the first to talk. "I'm exhausted. I think we'll order room service and spend the night in."

"We'll probably do the same," Gabi said, and Sophia nodded. "Let's try to make sure we see each other tomorrow before getting off, okay?"

"Of course," Major said, and then he and Violet headed toward the elevator, while Gabi and Sophia took the stairs.

Several hours later, and the remains of dinner belatedly

delivered by a harried room service guy piled on top of the small desk, Gabi wearily placed the phone back into its cradle.

"That was the last of them," she sighed and flopped down onto the bed, giving in, for the moment, to exhaustion.

"Any damage?" Sophia asked from where she sat cross-legged on her bed.

"Out of eight clients onboard, six were nowhere near the accident," Gabi answered. Lying on her back, she absently traced the lines of the ceiling tiles with her eyes. "They were released quickly and can get off whenever they want tomorrow." She pushed herself up, rubbing her eyes with the heels of her palms. "Unfortunately, two had been watching the parasailing, the Mitchells and the Garcia family. Mr. Garcia told me his youngest, Javier, is a bit traumatized."

"I don't blame him," Sophia replied softly.

Gabi pulled her hands away from her face and looked at Sophia. Dressed in red sweatpants and a Taylor Swift concert T-shirt, with her shoulder-length hair pulled into pigtails, she looked much younger than thirty-five.

Gabi, on the other hand, felt much older. "Me neither," she said, twisting her ponytail around her fingers. "Thankfully, Mrs. Umai and her daughter hadn't finished hiding all of their cruise ducks, so I arranged with her to leave one outside of the Garcia's cabin tonight for Javier to find in the morning. Hopefully, it'll cheer him up."

"Aww, that's sweet," Sophia said. "I love the tradition of hiding rubber ducks on ships. Especially when people theme them, like for the holidays. I was hoping I'd find one on this trip, but now…"

A moment passed, with each lost in their own thoughts.

"Gabi?" Sophia finally asked, breaking the silence. "Maybe we should go to sleep."

Gabi looked at her friend and co-worker. Tears burned

behind her eyes, and she blinked rapidly to prevent them from falling.

Sophia darted over from her bed and put an arm around Gabi's shoulders, hugging her. "Gabi-doll, go to sleep. It's been a long day. We're both exhausted. You sent your aunt and your sister emails this morning, and they haven't responded. What's the point in trying again at this hour?"

Gabi hugged Sophia back. She appreciated her friend's efforts. "You're probably right. I'm just going to check once more. After that, I promise I'll go to sleep."

"Okay. I'm here if you need to talk."

"Thanks, Soph."

Sophia went back to her bed and got under the covers. Gabi quickly changed into her pajamas and turned off the small light above her twin bed. Then she grabbed her phone from the bedside stand and opened her e-mail. Her sister had finally e-mailed her back. The subject line read: "Biopsy results."

4

Gabi felt more excited than she'd ever felt before. Practically skipping down the hall towards the hospital room, she yelled ahead to her father. "Daddy. Daddy, I figured it out." Her momentum halted abruptly as she collided with a man carrying bed sheets. Her nose wrinkled as she pushed past the man and the gross-smelling sheets. "Daddy, I figured it out," she repeated and then stopped. Daddy wasn't there.

"Gabi? Gabi. Gabi!" Sophia's voice slowly penetrated Gabi's mind. "Gabi, stop yelling."

"Huh? What?" Gabi responded in confusion. The line between dream and reality was still blurry, though the dream was receding quickly.

"You were calling for your dad."

Gabi tried to focus on Sophia's face. Sophia's hair was messy, her dark-brown eyes still sleepy.

"You kept yelling *daddy*."

"I was dreaming," Gabi said as the last images of the dream fading from her mind. "I guess about my dad." She pulled her knees to her chest and rubbed her eyes.

Sophia let a moment of silence pass. "Gabi," she asked

hesitantly. "You never talk about your dad. You told me he was dead when we first met, but you never said much beyond that. Yesterday, you said he'd been a cop. I guess I knew that, but is that how he died?"

Gabi picked up her phone to see the time—7:45. Her alarm would be going off in half an hour. She looked back at Sophia.

"No… He had cancer."

Gabi watched as Sophia's eyes widened. "Aunt Maggie. She's your dad's sister."

"Yep. And…and it's the same type of cancer. Pancreatic." Though she spoke the last word softly, it filled up the room.

"Oh, Gabi. I'm so sorry." Sophia pulled her bed cover off, clearly intending to step across to hug her.

"No, Soph, don't. Not now. I just can't right now. We have to meet with the FBI in a little while, and I'm so tired. I can't." Tears threatened to spill, but Gabi fought to keep them back. *Nothing. I feel nothing,* she repeated to herself.

"It's okay. I understand. I really do. Whenever you're ready."

"You know what? Since I'm up now and we still have a little time, I think I'm going to go work out." Gabi threw on the sweats she'd been wearing last night before bed, along with the tee she always had in her carry-on in case her luggage was lost. She almost smiled at the surprise on Sophia's face as she laced up her sneakers. She rarely worked out, but at that moment, it felt like exactly what she needed.

"You work out? Where's Gabi, and what have you done with her?" Sophia joked, though Gabi could hear the empathy in her voice.

"Ha-ha, very funny," she said, careful not to slam the door behind her.

In the gym, Gabi attacked the elliptical with vigor. After only fifteen minutes, her shirt and hair were soaked with sweat. Twenty minutes later, with her calves trembling, she finally slowed her stride to a stop and stepped off. She walked over to the water cooler at the back of the gym and gulped down two paper cups of water before grabbing a clean towel off a nearby rack and mopping up the sweat that dripped from her chin.

Finally ready to head back to the cabin, Gabi threw the towel into a bin and turned to leave. She stopped short in surprise. On the elliptical she had left was the redheaded woman she knew to be Connor's wife.

Really? Gabi thought. *Her husband just died in a freak accident, and she's in the gym exercising?* Gabi quickly reprimanded herself. She had taken to the gym because she couldn't deal with all the crap that was going on in her life, so why shouldn't Connor's wife do the same? Still, it seemed odd. With a sideways glance at the woman as she passed, Gabi left the gym and returned to her cabin to shower and change.

A half hour later, she and Sophia darted upstairs to the breakfast buffet to grab some food to go—fruit and cottage cheese for Sophia, a bagel with cream cheese and smoked salmon for Gabi—and then raced down five flights of stairs to get to the Neptune Theater, where they were required to be at 10:30 for their meeting with the FBI.

Gabi didn't know what she'd been expecting, but she was surprised when they walked into the theater and saw close to 100 other people sitting there already.

"Somehow, I don't think this is gonna be over quickly," Gabi said after giving their name and room number to a tall man in a dark suit, who indicated which section of the theater they should sit in.

"The real men in black," Sophia whispered to Gabi, her chin tilted down so the sound wouldn't carry back to the FBI agent who'd ushered them in.

"Now if Will Smith would make an appearance, I wouldn't mind the wait," Gabi whispered back, and they both giggled.

"Bruce Devonshire," a second man in a dark suit called out. The man was standing on the stage with the curtain closed behind him. When a person who must have been Bruce Devonshire approached, the man in the suit pointed to the stage stairs. Once Bruce was on the stage, the man led him behind the curtain.

"If they're doing one person at a time, this could take half the day," Sophia commented.

Gabi ate her bagel silently, watching the other people in the theater. Those with friends or family sat with their heads together, whispering. Others sat alone, some with books, others simply looking off into space, waiting to be called. When she turned her attention to the two FBI agents by the doors, she had to stifle a nervous giggle as she wondered whether anyone ever tried to joke with them by asking for Agent Mulder or Scully. Judging by the dour expression on both agents' faces, she doubted they'd appreciate such a joke.

"Gabi, you okay?" Sophia asked, clearly responding to the strangled sound Gabi had made when she forced herself not to laugh.

"Huh? Yeah, just thinking. Hey, I didn't tell you who I saw in the gym this morning, did I?"

"No, you didn't. Dish," Sophia replied eagerly, never one to pass up a bit of gossip.

Gabi glanced around quickly and lowered her voice to even more than the whisper they were already using. "Connor's wife."

"You didn't!"

"Shh. Yes, I did. She came in right before I left and was working out like the devil himself was after her."

"Guess she's not too broken up about Connor," Sophia said.

"I don't know…" Gabi shrugged. "Maybe she needed to work off her emotions."

"Did she look upset? Like she'd been crying or hadn't slept?" Sophia asked.

Gabi thought for a moment. "Hard to say, honestly. She definitely looked like she was focused on something, but whether it was her exercise or thinking about something else, I couldn't say. I don't think she looked like she'd been crying, but I really only got a quick look at her. I didn't think she'd appreciate me staring."

"Sophia Viscardi," the agent on the stage called.

"That's you." Gabi nudged Sophia. "That wasn't too bad," she added after looking at the time on her cell.

"Hopefully you'll be next," Sophia said and headed for the stage.

About half the people who'd been in the theater when Gabi and Sophia arrived were now gone, but new people had replaced them. Twirling a strand of hair with her fingers, she surveyed faces, looking for anyone she might know. She spotted a few people she recognized but no one she knew well enough to wave hello to.

She relaxed into the chair, letting her head fall back and closed her eyes. An image of Connor mid-fall, leg hooked around a wire, flashed across her closed eyelids, and she jerked upright, blinking rapidly to dislodge the image. But with nothing else to do, her eyes soon closed again. As the minutes ticked by, a series of memories came to mind—her dad in his police uniform, her dad and Aunt Maggie laughing at some childhood joke, Aunt Maggie in the kitchen cooking her delicious eggplant spread for Hanukkah, her dad in a hospital bed with tubes and wires attached to his arms, the fear in Aunt Maggie's face when she told Gabi the doctor suspected cancer. Warm tears slipped down her cheek, and she used her sleeve to wipe them away.

"Damn it," she whispered to herself. "Get ahold of yourself, Gabriella."

Fidgeting in her seat and tugging on her hair with one hand, Gabi glanced at her phone. It had been about twenty minutes since Sophia had been called up. *Come on,* she thought.

As if in answer to her unspoken plea, an agent pushed through the stage curtain. "Gabriella Feraru."

Gabi darted out of her seat and walked quickly toward the stage. *Let's get this over with.*

She followed the FBI agent past the heavy, red velvet curtain. Immediately, she noticed Sophia at the far right of the stage, talking animatedly to the FBI agent who sat across from her.

The stage had been divided into three partitions that were spaced far enough apart to give a semblance of privacy. Each space had three "walls" made of what appeared to be thick cardboard, and Gabi stifled her impulse to touch one.

She followed the black-suited agent to the middle space, where another agent in a black suit sat behind a metal folding table, typing loudly into his laptop.

As she entered, the man stopped typing and stood, waving his hand to indicate she should take a seat. "I'm Agent Robert Jacks. Thank you for meeting with us today."

Gabi faltered a moment as she looked at Agent Jacks. He looked to be in his mid-thirties and would not be out of place in a *Men of the FBI* calendar. His dark-blond hair was cut close to his head, not quite a buzz cut but just shy of one. His eyes were green, and the laugh lines around his eyes told her he wasn't always so stiff.

"You are one of the agents invited on this familiarization

cruise?" He said the word familiarization as if it were a foreign word he'd only recently learned.

"Travel advisor."

"Sorry?"

"I'm a travel advisor, not a travel agent."

"I see." Though he didn't smile, Gabi could see her correction amused him.

She sighed. Now was not the time and place to explain the difference. "Yes, I'm one of the travel advisors invited on this FAM. Advisors usually qualify by selling—"

"Yes or no answers will do, Miss Feraru. You witnessed Connor Foley's death?"

"Please call me Gabi," she said and flipped her hair over her shoulder. "And yes."

This time Agent Jacks did smile, for a moment. "Can you tell me why you were at the back of the boat at the time of the incident…Gabi?"

"I was at the *aft* of the *ship*," Gabi said, emphasizing the words to indicate Agent Jacks wasn't using the correct wording, "to watch the parasailing. I was also scheduled to participate at a later time."

"Was Mr. Foley the first to go?"

Gabi didn't answer at first, and Agent Jacks looked up from his laptop. "Miss… Gabi?"

"Surely you already know the answer to that question," she said, stifling a yawn.

"I realize some of these questions may seem trivial to you, but it's important that we get a consensus from all the witnesses. Please, *Gabi*," he said, emphasizing her name, "was Mr. Foley the first person to go parasailing?"

"No, he was the second."

"Who was first?"

"Seriously?" Gabi snapped, all thoughts of flirting

suddenly gone. "There's no way every single person you spoke to before me didn't give you the exact same answer."

"Miss Feraru, please just answer my questions."

Oh, it was back to Miss, was it? she thought. "Agent Jacks, I'm happy to answer your questions. But please don't waste my time with things you already know."

Agent Jacks cleared his throat, and the warmth in his eyes dimmed. "Did you notice anything unusual when Mr. Davidson went up?"

Gabi closed her eyes and tried to picture what she'd seen. "Stefan looked a little nervous, but who wouldn't, right? The whole thing seemed normal to me. But I've never seen anyone parasail before, so I'm not sure I'm qualified to say what is or isn't usual."

"What about when it was Mr. Foley's turn? Tell me what you saw then."

She summarized everything she'd seen for Agent Jacks, pausing towards the end as she pictured Connor's last moments. "And then he fell," she said softly, her voice catching.

Agent Jacks gave her a moment to collect herself. "You said he looked lopsided. What do you mean by that?"

She searched for the right words. "I can't really explain, but it looked more like he was dangling than hanging in the straps, if that makes any sense."

"Did you know Mr. Foley?"

"No."

Agent Jacks's eyes narrowed slightly. "Yet you refer to him as Connor?"

"The first time I ever saw him, which was on this cruise, I heard someone call him Connor. So that's how I thought of him." Gabi shifted uncomfortably in the metal folding chair.

"Were you alone watching the parasailing?"

"No. I was with my friend and co-worker, Sophia Viscardi."

Agent Jacks's eyebrows drew closer together as he glanced first at his laptop then back at her. "And?" he asked expectantly.

"And?" She wasn't sure what he was getting at.

"And who else was with you? Who were you speaking with?"

"Who else was I speaking to? We were surrounded by people. I'm sure I chatted with whoever was standing next to me at some point. I guess I also shared a conversation with Major and his wife Violet, who were behind us."

"Had you ever met Mr. Foley before?"

What the hell, Gabi thought as Agent Jacks changed direction yet again. She had been expecting him simply to ask about the accident and then let her go, but this felt much more like an interrogation. "Didn't I just say I didn't know him?"

"Yes, but had you met him before?"

"If you can call it a meeting, yes, I suppose we had. We sat at the same table at lunch yesterday."

"I see. And how well do you know George Thomas?"

Gabi's brow furrowed at the question. The name sounded familiar, but at the moment, she couldn't recall why.

"The man you call Major," Agent Jacks prompted.

Gabi's Spidey sense prickled. "Why are you asking about Major?"

"Please, Miss Feraru, answer the question."

"Not until you answer mine. I thought I was here to talk about the accident yesterday."

"Miss Feraru, for now, I will ask the questions. I assure you, I have a reason for everything I'm asking you. How well do you know George Thomas?"

"Major and I met last year on a fam trip in Jamaica. We've stayed in touch since then by e-mail and met again two days ago at the opening ceremonies for *Sea Fantasy*."

"You said before that the first time you saw Mr. Foley, you heard him referred to as Connor. Can you tell me when this was?"

Gabi searched Agent Jacks's face. These were not the questions she had expected to have to answer. What did he need all this background info for?

"Miss Feraru?"

"You don't think this was an accident, do you?" she asked, understanding more viscerally than ever before why people used the term, "like a lightbulb turning on."

A surprised look flashed across Agent Jacks's face.

"Despite all the episodes of *Law & Order* I'm sure you've watched and all the true-crime podcasts you've listened to, please don't assume you know what we're thinking."

"Condescending much? Not that it's any of your business, but my father was a detective. So, yeah, I know a little something about what to expect if you actually thought this was an accident. How about we cut through all the BS? I have a lot of work ahead of me, figuring out which of my clients have been affected by this event and who I have to talk down off the ledge. So what is it you really want to know?"

Agent Jacks rubbed a spot behind his right eye and huffed. "Right now, Miss Feraru, I want you to tell me about the first time you encountered Mr. Foley. As for whether we believe this was an accident or not, we're still trying to ascertain that. Your answers, whether you believe it or not, will help us."

Gabi suppressed an urge to huff back at Agent Jacks. "It was the first night of the cruise, at the inaugural party. He and a redheaded woman had an argument. She called him Connor."

"You witnessed Mr. Foley's argument with his wife?"

"Yes, and with her brother. He, his name is Brendan, said he'd kill Connor if he ever shoved his sister again," Gabi added.

Agent Jacks nodded, as if confirming something, and typed into his computer. "You also witnessed the altercation between Mr. Foley and Mr. Thomas, yes? Do you often find yourself in the middle of fights?"

"Let me guess... Your attempt at cop humor?" Gabi asked. "Listen, if you don't have anything else *new* to ask me, can I go?"

Agent Jacks picked up a bottle of water and took a sip, drawing out his reply for almost a full minute. "Tell me about that second altercation."

Gabi's annoyance turned to discomfort. She didn't like that Agent Jacks kept asking about Major.

"Do you need me to repeat the question, Miss Feraru?"

There was nothing for it. "Major came into the dining room and accused Connor of stealing his clients."

"And then?"

"You already know this," Gabi snapped.

Agent Jacks didn't respond, just cocked one eyebrow at her to let her know he was waiting.

"And then Major punched Connor and security dragged him out."

"Did Mr. Thomas say anything else?"

Gabi's nostrils flared, and she took a deep breath before answering. "He said that if Connor stole any more clients, he'd be a dead man."

"Who would be a dead man, Miss Feraru?"

"Connor."

Agent Jacks typed once more into his laptop. "Thank you, *Gabi*. You have been very helpful, and believe it or not, I appreciate your honesty with me." He fished a card out of his pocket and smiled. "Here's my card. If you think of anything, anything at all, please call me."

5

——————

A LITTLE MORE THAN a week passed in a blur. Despite being busier than ever with work and taking her aunt back and forth to the hospital for radiation and chemo treatments, Gabi couldn't shake the conversation with Agent Jacks from her thoughts. The last time she'd seen Major, the day they all departed the *Sea Fantasy*, he had seemed unbothered by the Fed's focus on his fight with Connor, but Gabi didn't like it.

Sitting in her aunt's room, a rough draft of a Kenya and Tanzania safari itinerary on her lap, she stared into space replaying Connor's death over in her mind.

"Did I fall asleep again?" Aunt Maggie's voice broke into Gabi's thoughts.

Gabi placed the itinerary she'd been ignoring on the floor and rolled her chair closer to Aunt Maggie's bed. Across the way, Alina looked up from her book. "Just for a little while," she said.

"You must be so bored, sitting there watching me sleep."

Alina pulled her chair closer and took Aunt Maggie's hand. "That's okay. We don't mind at all."

"We like sitting with you," Gabi added. "Besides, you

don't stay asleep for long, so we get to chat when you're awake. And when you're napping, I'm able to catch up on paperwork. Which, mind you, is much easier to do away from the office, where phone calls and Sophia's chatter can be distracting. It's all good."

Aunt Maggie gave them a small smile and tried to lick her lips but grimaced from the pain of the canker sores that had cropped up within days of starting radiation. "How have you been sleeping, Gabi? You look as tired as I feel," she said, her watery eyes narrowed with concern.

Gabi's throat constricted. Aunt Maggie was lying in bed in a thick flannel nightgown. In spite of the balmy June weather, she had a difficult time staying warm, and her normally husky voice sounded thin and listless to Gabi. The doctors said it was all side effects of the chemotherapy and radiation, both of which she'd started a week ago. Her skin was tight across her face, and her gray-white hair, which had already thinned with age, was wispier than ever. Yet, despite her obvious discomfort, Aunt Maggie showed more concern over Gabi's lack of sleep than she did about her own condition. Gabi had to blink back tears at the thought of losing her.

"I'm okay, Aunt Maggie, really. I'm more worried about you."

"Gabi's never been a great sleeper anyway," Alina said. "Don't worry about anyone but yourself."

Gabi smiled at Alina gratefully, glad that her sister was backing her up. They'd really only come to be friends a year and a half ago, after a lifetime of butting heads.

Aunt Maggie caught the look between the two and patted Gabi's hand. "Gabi, I'm sure seeing that man's death was traumatic enough. You don't also need to worry about me. I don't know how many times I have to tell you girls. I'm not afraid anymore, and you don't need to be either."

"Don't talk like that," Gabi said, pulling her hand away from Aunt Maggie and standing up. "You sound like you're giving up. The doctor said there's a chance you can survive this. Concentrate on that instead of this whole, 'whatever will be, will be' crap."

"Gabriella," her sister warned.

"What?" Gabi rounded on Alina. "This whole 'I'm not afraid of dying' is BS. She has to fight."

"*She* is right here," Aunt Maggie interjected, annoyance clear, despite the weakness in her voice. "And I'm not giving up. That's why I'm doing this…" She waved her hand as best she could at the spot below her collarbone to indicate the chemo port. A vitamin K deficiency the doctors were struggling to contain caused her hand to tremble violently. "But if I *had* decided I was done with fighting, that would be my right."

Spent, Aunt Maggie dropped her hand back onto the bed and tried to take deep breaths. Alina quickly reclaimed her aunt's hand, holding it until the trembling subsided.

"Shh, Aunt Maggie. It's okay," Alina said, stroking the back of the hand she held. "Gabi understands. Don't you, Gabi?"

Looking at Aunt Maggie still trying to catch her breath, Gabi acquiesced but gave her sister a look that said they'd be finishing the conversation later.

Aunt Maggie spoke again. "You need to be realistic. Yes, the doctors gave me a chance, but it's only a ten percent chance. Those are slimmer odds than they gave your dad—"

"But Dad died years ago. They have better treatments now." Gabi cringed at the whine in her voice. "I… I just don't want you to give up. I need you." Tears stung the corners of her eyes. "Please keep fighting."

"Okay, Gabriella. Okay."

Several minutes passed, and the sisters assumed their aunt

had fallen asleep again. But she opened her eyes and looked at Gabi. "Speaking of fighting... Tell us more about that man who died. It's like a real-life movie thriller. Alina, help me sit up."

Once upright, Aunt Maggie paused to catch her breath again, and when she spoke, Gabi could hear the breathlessness in her voice. "I believe you were saying something about a fight before I dozed off."

Though she'd been home for over a week, she hadn't had a chance to give both her sister and aunt a complete retelling of the events from the *Sea Fantasy's* inaugural sailing.

"The one with Major," Alina prompted. "I can't imagine him losing his temper like that."

"Believe me, it was as shocking to me too."

"I don't remember the details. Can you tell me again?" Aunt Maggie asked.

"Right, so the man who died, Connor, sat at the same table as Sophia and me at lunch the day he died. And boy, was he rude! But then Major came storming in, accused Connor of stealing his clients, and punched him, right in front of everybody. But that was right after... Oh shoot!"

Aunt Maggie's eyes popped open at Gabi's outburst. "I'm still awake."

"No, no. It's not that. I just remembered I forgot to tell the FBI about the altercation between Connor and the woman in the short-shorts and the one with his brother-in-law. How could I have forgotten? Both of them threatened Connor too. If the feds really don't think Connor's death was an accident, they should be looking at them, especially his brother-in-law, not Major."

"And Major is that nice older travel agent you met last year? The one who used to be a soldier?"

Gabi and Alina exchanged worried glances at Aunt

Maggie's questions, the same ones she'd asked several times already.

"Yes, that's him," Gabi said.

"A man in uniform, just like your dad." Aunt Maggie seemed on the verge of drifting into sleep.

"Yep, just like Dad," Gabi said, squeezing Aunt Maggie's hand. Then she continued, more to herself than anyone else. "And he's innocent, I'm sure of that. But that Brendan, he's another story. A real thug."

"Then you should tell the FBI," Aunt Maggie said softly before succumbing to sleep.

Gabi and her sister sat quietly for a few minutes. Then Alina stood and put her book in her bag. "I've got to go pick up the kids. Maybe we'll talk later? And I'll see you back here tomorrow."

"Yep, see you."

They waved good-bye, still awkward with each other even after more than a year of developing their bond.

Gabi stayed a little longer, gazing at her aunt's thin face and rubbing her thumb over the back of her aunt's hand. She blinked away the tears that threatened to fall. "Okay, Aunt Maggie, you sleep now," she whispered. "You need your rest so you can fight this thing." She swallowed a sob. "I can't lose you." Gabi kissed her aunt gently on the forehead then gathered her papers off the floor.

As she exited the room, she glanced back over her shoulder at her aunt lying in bed. Aunt Maggie looked so much smaller than her five foot seven inches. Gabi's heart skipped a beat. The last time she'd seen her dad, she hadn't known it would be for the last time.

～

It took Gabi a little over twenty minutes to get from her home to the Best in Travel office. At a time when most advisors worked from home, her boss insisted on keeping the office open. The agency was one of five storefronts on the east side of Willow Road, a short stretch of road that only spanned the distance between the parallel North and South Avenues, which were the largest roads running through the downtowns of several area townships. It was located immediately next to the train station, and it wasn't unusual for someone returning from a day's work in New York City to stop into their office in the early evening to ask about vacation planning.

As Gabi turned the key to let herself into the office, a marmalade cat darted across the office to hide underneath Sophia's desk.

"It's okay, Bugsy," Gabi crooned reassuringly. "I'm here to make a phone call and do some paperwork. I won't bother you."

Bugsy was a feral kitten that Sophia, Gabi, and Lewis were slowly trying to rehabilitate, but he was still skittish around people. It didn't help that Lewis, who had actually rescued him, was rarely, if ever, in the office. Before settling down at her desk, Gabi checked Bugsy's water and food bowls. Both were full, so Gabi knew Sophia had stopped by earlier in the day to spend some time with him.

When Gabi had entered, Bugsy had been sleeping on her desk, which was currently bathed in early afternoon sun. When he'd bolted, he'd sent papers flying, among them the folder that contained all her *Sea Fantasy* paperwork. Gabi quickly scooped up all the scattered papers and plunked down into her chair, an ergonomic affair she had splurged on after selling her first commission-rich river cruise. Nine years old, the chair's arms were frayed and tattered from rubbing under her desk, but it was still wonderfully comfortable.

Luckily, none of the contents of the folder had been dislodged. Having settled cross-legged into the chair, Gabi shuffled through the folder to find Agent Jacks's business card. She'd been meaning to call him ever since she'd remembered the other fights a couple of days ago.

She picked up her desk phone and began to dial the number but stopped halfway. "What do you think, Bugsy?" she asked the kitten, who stared at her uncertainly from under Sophia's desk on the other side of the office. "Should I call Agent Jacks? If they've already determined it was an accident, which it probably was, then he doesn't need to hear from me."

She unfolded her legs and stood. Careful to keep her distance from the kitten, she paced the six or so feet between her desk and the office's glass front. "But if they're still investigating and they think Major was involved, then letting them know about that woman and Brendan would be a good thing, right?"

Gabi paused in her pacing and tapped her fingers against her lips. "On the other hand, do I really want to get any more involved than I already am? I mean, I didn't know Connor, and let's be honest, I suppose I don't know Major that well either." Gabi whirled to face the kitten, who pulled back in alarm. "But Major wouldn't do anything like this. I just know it." She stared at the kitten who, this time, stared back. "My dad used to tell me, follow the facts but trust your gut. I'm gonna call."

Gabi returned to her desk, picked up the phone, and dialed Agent Jacks's number.

After two rings, he picked up. "This is Agent Jacks. How may I help you?"

"This is Gabi, Gabriella Feraru. I was on the *Sea Fantasy* when Connor Foley died."

Agent Jacks didn't skip a beat. "Yes, Gabi, I remember. How are you?"

Gabi felt her pulse quicken when she heard he remembered her but quickly pushed the flush of pleasure aside. She had business to attend to. "I'm well. I remembered something that I forgot to mention before."

"Of course. I'm so glad you called. Is this about something you saw during the incident?"

"No, before it happened, actually. It was at lunch that day."

Agent Jacks paused for a moment. "I see. Do you have more information regarding George Thomas's attack on Connor Foley?"

Shoot, Gabi thought. They were still looking at Major as a suspect. "No, this occurred before Major—sorry, George—showed up."

"I see."

Gabi thought she detected a trace of confusion in his voice.

"Go on."

"Before Major came to the table, Connor got into a fight with some woman who said he owed her money. She was pissed off, big time. And after that, he had words with his brother-in-law, Brendan."

"Is that Brendan O'Malley?"

"I don't know his last name, only that his first name is Brendan and he's the brother of Connor's wife. He's a big guy, very muscular."

"And what exactly happened?" Agent Jacks sounded interested, and Gabi was surprised that no one had mentioned the incidents to the FBI beforehand.

"Well, first, this woman came over and said Connor owed her money. She didn't say how much. Connor said he didn't and told her she was never going to get anything from him. The way he said it made it sound like a threat, like leave me alone or I'll make you kind of thing. She gave it right back to him and told him he was going to pay up one way or another."

"Do you know what the name of this woman is?"

"He called her Tanya. That's all I know. I didn't recognize her, and I don't remember seeing her again, which means she probably wasn't a travel advisor."

"I'll definitely look into this. And Brendan? Tell me about that."

"They were arguing. Brendan was saying that he and Connor were going into business together, and Connor wasn't having it. Right before Major turned up, both Connor and Brendan had stood up. It looked like they were about to start fighting."

"Did it come to blows?"

"No, Major got there first. But before that, Connor said very clearly that they were never going into business together, and Brendan replied something about Connor ending up dead if he wasn't careful or something like that."

"Let me get this straight, Gabi. You're saying Brendan O'Malley threatened Connor Foley?"

"Again, I don't know if those were the exact words he used, but yes, that was the gist of it."

"Thank you very much, Gabi. This has all been very helpful. Do you have anything else to add?"

"Well, yes, but I don't know how helpful it will be."

"Every little bit of information you can provide is helpful, Gabi."

"The morning that all of this happened, I overheard an argument between Connor and somebody else, but I never saw who the person was, though now I wonder if it was that Tanya woman. I was heading to the bathroom when I heard a man yelling at someone else not to threaten him. By the time I got to the corner, the other person was out of sight, but Connor was there. I really don't remember exactly everything he said, but I do remember that he accused this other person of thinking they were better than him. Then he said something about 'this,' whatever 'this' was, ending when he decided it was over, and not the other way around."

"Could you hear this other person's voice at all?"

"No, whoever it was wasn't yelling the way Connor was."

"Could you tell if it was a man or a woman?"

"No, I'm sorry. All I heard was Connor."

"Okay, well, thank you again for calling, Gabi. I do appreciate it."

"Agent Jacks, may I ask you something?" Gabi hoped he'd be more forthcoming than the first time they'd met.

"Of course. You can ask anything, but I can't promise I'll be able to answer."

"On the ship, you said the FBI was still investigating Connor's death and no determinations about whether it was an accident had been made yet."

"The FBI always investigates a death on a cruise ship, especially such a violent death. Honestly, Connor Foley's death was suspicious from the start."

"I see. And…has anything been determined? Was it an accident?"

"I can't give you any details, but we have issued a statement saying that we do not believe that Connor Foley's death was an accident."

Gabi exhaled sharply and tugged on her ponytail. "So, someone killed him?" she blurted out, unable to keep the shock out of her voice.

"That's really all I can say right now."

"But that doesn't make sense." Gabi thought furiously for a minute. "You are implying that someone would have had to sabotage Connor's parasailing rig. That's crazy."

"Why would you draw that conclusion?" Agent Jacks asked.

"It's the only thing that makes sense. Somehow, someone did something to make the parasail rigging break so Connor would fall. But I don't see how that's possible. I watched the crew check his rig and give it a thumbs-up."

"You make a pretty good detective for a travel agent—sorry, travel advisor."

"My dad was a detective. I guess I picked up some tricks from him."

"Listen, I'm really not supposed to say anything, but I'll say this. With his military background, Mr. Thomas has the expertise needed to have done this, but I'll make sure we look into Brendan O'Malley's background as well."

Gabi's stomach dropped. What would Major's military experience have to do with anything?

As if he could hear the wheels in Gabi's head turning, Agent Jacks asked, "How well do you know George Thomas?"

"He's a friend. Though we've only known each other a year, I feel like I know him pretty well. I'm telling you, Major is a good guy. He wouldn't do something like this."

"In all of the time that you've known each other, did he talk to you about Connor Foley or about how the man might have stolen his clients?"

Gabi paused at the reminder that Major hadn't confided in her. "No, he never did, but that doesn't mean he was nursing some murderous plot that he didn't want anyone to know about. Besides, he seemed as upset with Stefan Davidson as he did with Connor."

"Really? Did Mr. Thomas attack Mr. Davidson too?"

"You already know the answer to that. But I'm telling you Major was upset that Stefan and SeaCirque wasn't doing anything to stop Connor from poaching his clients or to punish him."

"So, if Mr. Davidson wasn't prepared to stop Mr. Foley, wouldn't that give Mr. Thomas a reason to do it himself?"

"Listen, Agent Jacks. I'm not stupid. I know what you're getting at, but I don't believe it for a second. What I do believe is that something was going on between Connor and his brother-in-law. And I most definitely believe that his brother-in-law is more than capable of killing someone."

"Believe it or not, Gabi, I respect your insights and really do appreciate this phone call. I assure you we will look into this woman Tanya and Mr. O'Malley, and if you think of anything else, please do not hesitate to call me."

Gabi stared at the office phone long after she had hung up. *Could she be wrong about Major?* He had definitely seemed angry enough to kill someone that day. She was usually a pretty good judge of character, but she'd been wrong about people before. Was she defending a guilty man? Her gut told her he was innocent, but she honestly couldn't be 100 percent sure.

6

____

"Poor Major," Sophia said, rescuing a margarita from BJ's overburdened hands. Gabi and Alina followed suit, each taking a beer from him as he sat down at the table.

"Who's Major? And why is he poor?" BJ asked, taking a sip of his old fashioned.

"He's the travel advisor from that ship they were on. The FBI thinks he killed that guy who was on it with them." Justin filled BJ in on the brief conversation he'd missed while getting the first round of drinks at the bar.

"He's not just some random guy though," Gabi added. "He's a friend, and I don't think that he killed anyone."

It was the foursome's monthly trivia night at the local pub, and the various teams were settling in. Maxine, the host, was making her way toward the front of the pub.

"Are we really only four people tonight?" Gabi asked. Usually Sophia or BJ, Gabi's unrepentant and so-far unsuccessful matchmakers, brought someone with them that they were hoping would both hit it off with her and help them win the night. That was how Justin had joined the team. While there'd been no chemistry beyond friendship between her and Justin, he had been a great addition to the team, and they now won more often than they lost.

"I figured you had enough going on, what with Aunt Maggie," Sophia answered.

"Meaning, you've been moody and at times a real bee-atch lately, and who would want to date that?" BJ added.

"Screw you," Gabi replied. "At least my socks match."

BJ stuck his tongue out at Gabi, who replied in kind.

"Everyone ready?" Maxine spoke into the microphone in front of her. "We've got sixteen teams tonight, so we'll do twenty-five questions instead of twenty. We'll start off with an easy one. Who wrote *The Prince*?"

Heads lowered, and the sound of whispers and pencils on paper filled the room.

"Oh, it's that guy. They even made an adjective out of his name," Gabi whispered then looked as Justin penciled in Machiavelli on their answer sheet.

"I'm so glad you and Gabi didn't hit it off," BJ said, clapping Justin on the back. "Speaking of you, my dear… I want to hear about this Major guy. First of all, is he a friend or a *friend*?" BJ put the second friend in air quotes. "And second, why do the feds think he's a murderer? And, third, since when are you all into bad boys?"

"You're impossible, you know that?" Gabi retorted. "Major is a married, 70-something year old Air Force veteran. So, no, he's not a *friend*." Gabi made her air quotes as sarcastic as she could.

"Who is Stefani Joanne Angelina Germanotta?" Maxine asked.

"That's easy," Sophia, who was their team's pop culture expert, said, grabbing the answer sheet from Justin and scribbling in Lady Gaga.

At the same time, BJ rephrased his second question to

Gabi. "So, anyway, why do you think the feds think he's guilty?"

"I want to hear this too," Sophia said.

"Basically, because they told me so. I called Agent Jacks earlier today because I'd forgotten to tell him about Connor's fight with some woman who claimed he owed her money and his fight with his brother-in-law. I also told him about an argument I'd overheard between Connor and someone else in a hallway."

"Oh, I never mentioned those fights either," Sophia said. "It totally slipped my mind when they were asking all those questions."

"Question number three," said Maxine. "What country has the oldest flag in the world?"

The foursome quieted down as they discussed the possibilities. They all agreed that a country somewhere in the Middle East made the most sense and eventually settled on guessing it was Turkey.

"Okay, so you called the FBI…" BJ prompted.

"And they actually told you that your friend was a suspect? That's surprising," Justin said.

"Not in so many words, but Agent Jacks did imply that it was Major's military background that made him such a good suspect."

"Oh, that's weird. What would military experience have to do with anything?" BJ asked.

At the same time, Justin said, "Hmm, what type of experience would someone have in the military that non-military people don't?"

"Guns?" Sophia said.

"Sure, he probably knows more about guns than the average person, but Connor wasn't shot," Gabi replied.

"What about explosives?" Justin said. "That seems like something someone in the military might learn about."

"That's true," Gabi answered slowly.

"Yeah, but we'd have seen an explosion, no?" Sophia said. "I mean, wouldn't an explosion have been obvious? And wouldn't it have taken off his head or something?"

"I don't know… In spy movies, they use explosives to make tiny holes in steel doors and stuff," BJ offered.

"Yeah, but that's in the movies. How much of that stuff is real?" Gabi said.

"I don't know. Everything I know about explosives I learned from TV and the movies," BJ said.

"Don't look at me. I'm with him," Justin said, pointing his thumb at BJ.

"Question five. What color is an octopus's blood?"

Justin pushed the paper to Gabi, who was the team's animal lover. Gabi had actually heard this question on a cruise ship before, so she knew the answer was blue and quickly wrote that down.

Then she thought more about the possibility that an explosive could have been used to break the parasailing rigging. While it made sense, she didn't know if such a thing was actually possible. But if explosives were involved, she understood better why the feds were looking at Major. As former military, he might know a thing or two about the stuff.

The question remained in her mind the rest of the evening though the conversation turned to BJ's latest boyfriend and Justin's new job. The next morning, in the office, Sophia and Gabi nursed their trivia pride over their loss the night before. They'd gotten four wrong, including the question about the world's oldest flag, which had stunned everyone in the room by being Denmark, and lost by one question. Their first-world pity party was only broken up when one of Sophia's clients showed up unexpectedly to discuss her upcoming honeymoon.

Gabi turned on her computer and tried to concentrate on learning more about river cruising. Though she'd been hearing about river cruises for several years—and, really, who hasn't seen a Viking river cruise commercial—she'd never actually sold one. But a growing interest in them from both older and family clients had prompted her to finally try to learn more about the different cruise lines and European rivers

Despite her desire to complete the program that day, Gabi couldn't stop her mind from wandering. After reading the same question three times, she accepted she was not going to be able to finish anytime soon. She saved her progress, logged out, and was about to check on the status of some overdue commissions she'd been tracking when the phone rang.

"Hello, Best in Travel. This is Gabi. Where can I help you escape to?"

"Hi Gabi, this is John Clarke from SeaCirque Cruise Line. We met briefly on the *Sea Fantasy*. I'm helpin' out some of Jill's clients while she's on maternity leave."

"Of course. It's nice to hear from you. How's Jill doing? I guess since you're calling, she's already on leave?"

"She's good. She's not out yet, but soon. She said she'll be givin' you a call before she goes. But I wanted ta call and say hi, plus I'd like ta invite you to Baltimore for a two-night trip to see the new port facility."

"Oh, that's right. I forgot you guys were going to be sailing the *Sea Magic* from there next year. And that article in *Travel Trade Today* said you'd put a lot of money into a big renovation there. How much of it is actually ready?"

"You'd be stayin' at the new SeaCirque hotel, which is entirely done. Most of the entertainment venues will be open. Only the shopping concourse and amusement park won't be ready yet. But when it's all done, it'll be a great base for a pre- or post-stay in Baltimore."

As John was talking, Gabi remembered that Major lived close to Baltimore. She'd been thinking about him a lot since her phone call with Agent Jacks and had been meaning to call him. But she'd been putting if off. What do you say to someone who is a suspect in a murder? Hey, congrats on your new status as murder suspect! Maybe this port trip could be a great opportunity to see him and talk in person.

"When would this be?" Gabi asked.

"A week from this Friday, the weekend after July fourth. I know it's short notice, but I really hope you can attend."

"Okay, hold on a sec." Gabi flipped through her desk calendar. Marked in pencil on that Saturday was dinner with her sister's family, but she could reschedule that. "Okay, count me in."

"Terrific. I'll e-mail the official invitation ta you now. It has all the details about when and where. I look forward ta seeing you again, Gabi."

"Me too, and thanks." Gabi hung up, crossed out dinner with her sister from the calendar, and added Port of Baltimore trip in pen. Then she pulled up her contacts list and searched for Major's info.

Major lived in Bowie, a city about halfway between Baltimore and St. Andrews Air Force Base, where he had been stationed for fifteen years. The location gave him easy access to his friends still living on the base and the metropolitan offerings of a bigger city. Gabi dialed the 240 telephone number and waited for someone to pick up.

"Cruising Away, this is Major Thomas." Major sounded tired to Gabi.

"Hi Major, it's Gabi."

"Gabi! How ya' doin', gal?"

"I'm good. Been thinking about you lately and

wondering how you were doing. Then a few minutes ago, I got a call from SeaCirque about a two-day Baltimore port trip, and that seemed like a message from the universe that I should call. I'll be doing that Baltimore trip, and I'm hoping you are too. I'd really like to get together and talk."

"Well now, I wasn't plannin' on going, but I would love to see you. You sound awful serious. Is everythin' okay? Your aunt, she hasn't…"

"No, no. She's okay. In and out of the hospital for her treatments." Gabi loved Major's thoughtfulness, and his southern roots shining through when he spoke didn't hurt. "The thing is…well…" Gabi didn't know how to proceed so decided blunt was best. "I spoke with the FBI yesterday and—"

"And they told you Connor's death wasn't an accident and I'm their number-one suspect," Major interrupted.

"Well, they didn't come right out and say it, but, yeah, they implied it. I tried to tell the agent I spoke with that there was no way you could've done it, but…" Gabi's voice trailed off.

"But why should they believe you?"

"Basically, yeah. Listen, I'd really love to get together. If you won't come to the port, I'll come to you after the trip. How's that sound?"

"You know what? I'll come, at least for one night. It's kinda a moot thing now, but I've been wanting to see what they were doin' with the place. And it'd be on their dime, so why not? I'll stay the Friday night and hang around for the tour on Saturday, and then Saturday night, you can come back to my place with me. Violet'd love to see you again. We'll have a nice dinner, and you'll stay the night and we can talk. Okay?"

"That sounds wonderful, but what did you mean it's a moot thing?"

"I'll explain when I see you in Baltimore. I've got to get back to work now, but I'll see you in a little over a week. You take care of yourself now."

The rest of the day passed quickly. After spending an hour making sure all her invoices for June were in order, her 1:00 appointment showed up. Kerry Cooper was an old high school acquaintance who was now married with three kids. Gabi was putting together a budget-friendly summer vacation to "someplace fun." They'd decided a five-day Bermuda cruise out of New York City would be a good fit, and though the commission wouldn't be huge, Gabi knew Kerry would come back to her for future vacations. And as her husband Mark had just made partner at his law firm, their budget would soon be going up.

On the Friday afternoon of her Baltimore trip, Gabi found herself running late after two client meetings she'd forgotten to reschedule. Though her 9:30 appointment with the Greenes had gone smoothly—she'd sold them on a 14-day land and river cruise package to China—her noon meeting did not. The Beaumonts were among Gabi's most affluent, albeit fussy, clients, and a one-hour meeting with them was never actually one hour. By 1:30, Gabi had to bring the meeting to a close, and they still hadn't touched on the entire Peru, Chile, and Easter Island trip they were planning. Mrs. My-Way-Or-the-Highway Beaumont had not been pleased when Gabi had stopped the meeting. Gabi had almost said something she'd never be able to take back, something along the lines of shoving the largest Easter Island Moai where the sun don't shine. With her nerves on edge, and a three-hour drive and what she could only imagine would be an awkward conversation with Major ahead of her, Gabi jumped into her bright blue Mini Cooper.

Despite the lateness of her departure, she stopped to say good-bye to Aunt Maggie. Gabi had become an expert at blocking out the mental image of her aunt and how bad the treatments made her look, so she could barely contain a grunt of dismay when she entered the room and was faced with reality. Though Aunt Maggie's trembling had subsided, her skeletal appearance had intensified. The circles under her eyes were darker, and her skin was stretched more tightly across her face than seemed possible. Gabi had pushed for her aunt to remain at home during her treatments, and for the first time, she wondered if that had been a mistake. And, for a fraction of a second, the possibility that her aunt might not actually survive slipped through her defenses.

"That bad?" Aunt Maggie tried for levity.

Gabi couldn't respond. She wanted to but was afraid if she opened her mouth, she'd vomit. Without a word, she turned and fled down the hall to the bathroom. Splashing cold water on her face, she tried to bring her emotions under control. Her eyes stung with unshed tears, but she refused to give in to them. Each day, Aunt Maggie seemed more resigned to her fate, and that didn't sit well with her. Anger was an emotion she was familiar with. It had sustained her for years after her father died and as her relationship with her mother got worse. She marched back to Aunt Maggie's room.

"You promised me you wouldn't give up. But you have, haven't you? I can see it in your eyes." When Aunt Maggie didn't respond right away, Gabi continued her tirade. "I knew it. You have. That's why you agreed to stay home, so you can die in your own bed."

"Gabi, shut up."

The shock of hearing those words from her aunt—words her aunt had never once said to her—stopped her cold.

"Come here."

Gabi obeyed, sitting softly on the bed next to her aunt.

"Don't pretend to know my thoughts, Gabriella. You have no right to tell me how I should be dealing with this illness. This is *my* life. And yes, my death, if that's what it comes to. You know as well as I do what the chances of survival are. If and when I decide to throw in the towel, you *will* have to deal with it. I don't expect you to like it, but I expect your support."

Gabi's thoughts reeled, and the silence between them lasted for what felt like several minutes. "I can't, Aunt Maggie," she finally said. "I refuse to accept…"

"Enough, Gabriella. Stop acting like a child."

Gabi flinched. The words echoed the haranguing she'd suffered at the hands of her mother from the moment her father died, when she was only twelve. Her gut reaction, to anything that brought up memories of her mother, was white-hot anger.

"Acting like a child?" she said, incredulous. "Because I don't accept that you dying is inevitable? I'll tell you what. If you have the right to tell me you're giving up, I have the right to tell you that's messed up."

"You're right, you do have that right. And I have the right to tell you that you *are* acting like a child. You're being selfish."

Gabi stood abruptly. She could feel the heat in her cheeks. "I'm being selfish? I want you to live, and I'm the one being selfish?"

"I appreciate that you want me to live, but you don't get to decide whether I live or die. You certainly don't get to tell me how I die. What you do get to do is be there for me, support me, and leave the decision making to me."

"In other words, stay out of your business, is that what you're saying?" Gabi was yelling now. "Fine."

"I wasn't finished." Aunt Maggie was struggling to speak, her own anger robbing her of vital energy, but Gabi barely registered her aunt's efforts. "You think I want to die? You think I don't remember what your father looked like at the end? What he went through? I didn't ask for this. But life never asks you what you want for dinner before shoveling a nasty surprise onto your plate. And you, pushing me to fight, fight, fight, every time you see me. I can't take on your fear *and* fight at the same time." Aunt Maggie finally stopped talking, unable to muster enough strength for any more words.

Gabi couldn't remember the last time she'd seen her aunt so angry. But anger often begets more anger, and it was easier to stay angry than to allow helpless grief in. "Fine, Aunt Maggie. You want me to leave the decision making to you. To stay out of your business. I can do that. I have enough to deal with at work, and right now I have a long drive ahead of me. I don't need to waste my time with you if you don't want me here. You think I don't have a right to care about whether or not you live or die? Fine."

She stormed out of the house, swiping at her eyes as tears came unbidden and unwanted.

7

———

IT WASN'T until she hit standstill traffic on I-95 South that Gabi allowed regret to pool in her stomach. She couldn't believe she'd told her aunt that being with her was a waste of time. She didn't feel that way at all. And the last thing she ever wanted to do was make things harder for her aunt. Aunt Maggie was right. Gabi was terrified. She couldn't imagine life without her.

She pulled her cell phone out of her purse and hit the short cut on her phone. Voicemail picked up. "Hi Aunt Maggie, it's me. I'm so sorry I yelled at you. I didn't mean what I said, any of it. I love you so much. I can't stand the thought of losing you. I don't mean to be selfish, but I need you in my life. Who else can I moan to about Mom? I know it's your life, but you're an important part of mine. Anyway, I wanted to say I'm sorry and I love you. I'll call later after I've gotten to Baltimore."

She hung up, and less than ten minutes later, traffic began to pick up. Within two hours, she was pulling into a parking spot at the Hotel de Cirque.

After checking in and picking up her guest packet, Gabi

stepped into an elevator and pushed the button for the four-teenth floor. As she waited for the doors to close, she noticed Brendan O'Malley enter the hotel lobby. Without thinking, she placed her hand on the elevator door to prevent it from closing and tracked his progress past the registration desk to the lobby bar. There, he approached a woman sitting with her back to the lobby. Gabi noticed the woman was wearing a short miniskirt. She hoped the woman would turn around.

"Oh, my dear, thank you for holding the door," a shrill voice said, and a woman in a garish yellow velour track suit stepped in front of Gabi, blocking her view of Brendan and the woman he was talking to.

Damn it, Gabi thought to herself, trying to crane her head around the woman without appearing rude.

"There's no one else waiting, dear," the woman said and pressed her pudgy finger against the close-door button. She didn't let go until the doors had closed.

Idly, Gabi watched as the woman attempted to fan herself with her room key card. *What is Brendan O'Malley doing here?* she wondered. *And who was he meeting with? Could that woman have been the same one from lunch the day Connor died?*

"…for the FAM?" Gabi caught the end of the woman's question and looked down at the registration packet in her hands that the woman was referring to. The woman held an identical packet.

"Oh, yes. Yes, I am. I'm pretty sure the hotel is only open to FAM participants. Oh!"

"Are you alright, dear?"

"Yes, I just remembered something," Gabi said absently, her thoughts circling her own words. Everyone here had to have been invited. She'd had to show her invitation at the parking lot entrance. That meant Brendan O'Malley could not have gotten as far as the lobby without an invitation as well. Like everyone else, he'd been invited. But why and by whom?

She chewed on that thought as the woman got off on the eighth floor. Six floors later, Gabi still hadn't figured out a possible answer to her question as she entered her room. As far as she knew, Brendan was not a travel advisor. He hadn't been on the *Sea Fantasy* as an advisor. It was her understanding that he'd been a loyal paying guest. Connor had been the travel advisor.

Gabi stopped unpacking as a thought struck her. Brendan had told her and Sophia that he and Connor were going into business together. Had he meant at Connor's travel agency?

Gabi sat heavily on the bed. Had Brendan taken over Connor's agency? If he had taken over the business and was continuing in the same line of work that Connor had specialized in, then he was probably planning on stealing more clients from Major. Could that be why Major seemed so tired?

Her phone rang.

"Hey darlin', they told me at registration that you'd checked in." Major's soft drawl sounded through the phone.

"Speak of the devil! I was just thinking about you. You'll never guess who I saw in the lobby."

"Now, now, it's too early for gossip. Get yourself cleaned up and changed and join me down in the lobby for a drink." Gabi thought Major's joviality sounded a little forced, but maybe he was making up for being tired. As far as she knew, he had put in a full day of work before making the one-hour drive to Baltimore.

"Okay, I need about a half hour," she said, glancing at her watch. "That'll still give us an hour before dinner. See you then."

Twenty minutes later, Gabi was trying to smooth out the

wrinkles in her black linen pants. Paired with a turquoise and fuchsia tunic that reached mid-thigh, she felt presentable but still comfortable. After a quick swipe of a brush through her hair—the event was too formal for her usual ponytail—and a dab of matte lipstick, she was ready to go. But first, she wanted to call Aunt Maggie again.

Val, the Jamaican home health aide she'd hired to help care for Aunt Maggie, picked up on the first ring.

"Hi Val. I tried to call a couple of hours ago but got my aunt's voicemail. Can she talk?"

"I had to take your auntie to the ER as she was having some difficulty breathing after you left. She's sleeping now."

"Is she okay now? We had a fight. Oh God, I didn't mean to upset her."

"Hush chile, she's fine. An' she's not angry wit' you anymore. These tings happen between family. I'll tell her you called."

"Okay. And Val? Tell her I love her."

Gabi sat on the edge of the bed, paralyzed with guilt. If Aunt Maggie had died that afternoon, Gabi never would have forgiven herself. She didn't ever want the last words between them to be in anger. Thankfully, there was no time for her to wallow. She wiped her eyes, grabbed her hotel room key, name badge, and evening purse. She stuffed her cell phone into the latter and then hurried towards the elevators.

She sighed in frustration when the first elevator to stop on her floor was packed and she had to let it go. Figured, since only two of the four elevators were in service. Patience had never been one of Gabi's virtues, and she was eyeing the door to the stairs when an elevator with room enough for one stopped.

She spied John Clarke in the corner of the elevator as she got on, but squished in as she was, she was not able to wave hello. Gabi waited to say hi after she was pushed out of the elevator by the flow of people getting off at the lobby. But by the time she turned around, there were only two elderly ladies left, slowly making their way out toward the end of a long path of advisors waiting for the open bar,

Thinking John must not have seen her get on, Gabi shrugged it off and headed for the bar, keeping an eye open for Major's buzz cut. A contortionist in a dark-purple mini tutu with bloodred tights and a black velvet corset moved through the crowd. She was bent backwards, walking with her hands and feet. A service tray for people's empty glasses was strapped to her stomach.

Gabi tracked the contortionist's progress for a moment before remembering she was supposed to be meeting Major. Her search came to an abrupt stop when she spotted Brendan O'Malley again. He was sipping from a bottle of beer as he chatted with John Clarke.

"Didn't your momma ever teach you it's not polite to stare," Major's drawl sounded in her ear. He gently guided her by the elbow away from the two men. "Not always safe either."

"I wasn't staring, not exactly," Gabi protested. "And what do you mean, not safe?" She tried to look over her shoulder, but Major blocked her line of sight.

Major didn't respond until he had led Gabi to the corner of the bar farthest from where Brendan and John were standing.

"What are you havin', Gabi?"

Gabi barely waited for Major to give their order to the bartender—a bellini for her, and for him, a scotch on the rocks—before revisiting her question.

"What do you mean, not safe? What is that man doing here?" She paused and lowered her voice. "And why am I suddenly sure you know what's going on?"

"Whoa there, missy. That's a lot of questions. Slow down." Major retrieved their drinks from the bartender and nodded to indicate they should move away from the crowds at the bar. Most of the sofas and easy chairs in the lounge were already taken, but some stools at a grouping of standing tables were still empty.

Gabi perched on the edge of a stool facing Major, and took a breath to speak, but he stopped her.

"Okay, okay. You're right. I can answer some of your questions. But I've got a ton of my own that I don't have answers for. And I wish I did, because then I'd be out of this whole mess."

She could hear the strain in his voice. Looking closer at him, she could see how tired he was. She was shocked; he'd aged at least ten years in the past three weeks. Dark circles contrasted sharply with his normally cheery blue eyes, and worry seemed to have etched a permanent furrow across his forehead. For a moment, Gabi regretted asking him to meet her at the hotel. She regretted her questions, and, if she was honest with herself, her prying. It was like what'd happened with Aunt Maggie all over again.

"You know what, Major? I'm sorry. I shouldn't be pushing. I'm sure you're getting enough grief from the FBI. You don't need this from me. I never should have made you come out here."

Major's loud snort surprised her.

"Aw, darlin'. Violet'd tell you no one can make this old dog do anything he doesn't want to. Truth is, I have been curious about what they were doing with this ol' port for a while. Plus, how could I pass up the chance to hang with you again."

Gabi had to smile at Major's attempt to use the word "hang," which, from the way he over emphasized it, was clearly not something he was used to saying.

"And when Violet found out about it, she was thrilled about you comin' for a night." Major took a sip of his scotch. "Besides, you never know what kind of business might get done at an event like this."

"Like getting to know John Clarke better?" Gabi pressed, her previous spasm of doubt having passed like a footstep beneath the waves.

"You sure are like a dog with a bone, gnawing away until you get to the marrow." Major smiled. "That's one of the things I like about you. You always want to get to the heart of things. Why things are the way they are and how to go about fixin' them when you can. Bet it makes you a great travel agent and an even better friend."

Gabi knuckled an errant tear from the corner of her eye, too embarrassed to respond. The two sipped their drinks. Above them, an aerialist was balanced precariously on one arm, her hand entwined in the fragile white ribbons that held her mid-air. Long lengths of silver-gray silk flowed away from her. Blown by an unseen fan, the silk panels undulated gently like gray clouds beneath the star-painted ceiling.

Gabi swiveled her stool to face the crowd gathered around the bar. Without thinking, she found herself scanning the area where she'd last seen Brendan O'Malley. She spotted John Clarke first. He was roughly in the same spot she'd last seen him, but now he was talking animatedly to two women, gesturing toward the small amusement park that lay on the other side of the hotel's windowed wall. While following his hand gesture, she spotted Brendan. Leaning with his back against the glass wall and his ankles crossed, he listened in apparent disinterest while Stefan Davidson spoke to him. From the intent look on Stefan's face, Gabi guessed they weren't exchanging pleasantries.

She slowly swiveled back around to Major, prepared to pretend she hadn't seen anything, but his eyes were already locked on Brendan and Stefan. She cleared her throat softly to catch his attention.

"John Clarke is not my new SeaCirque rep," he said quietly without looking at her. "Stefan is."

"Stefan? I didn't know he acted as a sales rep to advisors." Gabi tucked a stray strand of hair behind her ear, giving it a tug for good measure as she did so.

"Apparently, he likes to take on a few agents each year to work with personally." Major finally turned to look at her. "Connor was one of those."

"What?" Her surprise at the revelation caused her voice to spike. "But Connor was stealing…and now Stefan wants you…" Gabi tried to order her thoughts.

"He says it's his way of making things up to me," Major answered, his gaze back on Stefan and Brendan in the corner. "He didn't believe me when I told him what Connor was doing. Said he'd looked into it and found no evidence to back up my claims. But now with Connor gone, he wants bygones to be bygones. Or so he says." Major took a slow sip of his scotch, finally turning away from the two men. "I don't know."

"But if Stefan was working with Connor, there's no way he wouldn't have known what Connor had been doing. And what is going on with Brendan now?"

"Exactly," Major said.

Before the two could continue their conversation, they were distracted by an acrobat in a slinky black leotard rolling past them inside a large hoola hoop. He was spread-eagled inside the hoop, and she couldn't help but marvel at how well he managed to control his direction and speed without seeming to move at all. Shaking her head, she turned her attention back to Major.

"Do you know? What Brendan is doing?"

"From what I can tell, he's trying to take over Connor's

agency." Major's eyes tracked the acrobat as he rolled through the crowd. He sighed and his shoulders sagged ever so slightly. "But where Connor slid in quietly like a knife between the ribs, Brendan uses a massive club, making threats front and center."

Gabi inhaled sharply. "What kind of threats?"

Major didn't answer at first. He swirled the liquid in his glass, tinkling the ice cubes. She leaned forward when he began to speak, his voice barely carrying the distance between them. "He tells me that maybe I've got too much on my plate for a man my age. That I'm risking my health by continuing to work."

As Major told Gabi more about Brendan's threats, she had to keep her teeth clenched to prevent the string of curse words building up in her brain from spilling out.

"He tells me that at my age, my heart can't take a lot of stress and that he's only doing me a favor by taking work off my plate. He says that trying to get any of my clients back would be a bad idea, that it would be too much for me to handle." Major paused, his knuckles white against the glass he gripped. "He tells me that he'd hate to see Violet widowed too early."

Gabi didn't know what to say. She wanted to march straight across the room and punch Brendan. But she also wanted to reach out and take Major's hand, to offer him comfort. The barely contained tension rolling off Major held her back.

A low throat clearing brought the hotel lobby rushing back. Stefan stood beside them, two drinks in hand. "I hope I'm not interrupting."

"Oh, no," Gabi said, startled and flustered. "Major and I were talking about the port and this hotel. This is a great hotel you've built. I'm sure guests will love it, especially the families. That amusement park looks great." She couldn't keep the words from rushing out altogether.

"Gabi," Major said softly, his calm exterior back in place. He placed his hand on her shoulder to stop her babbling.

She quieted but eyed the two men warily. Stefan held a glass out to Major. "Let me buy you a drink."

Major raised an eyebrow and held up his hand to indicate that he already held a glass and that it was an open bar.

"It's Evan Williams, twenty-three years old. They don't pour it at the open bar," Stefan said.

Major placed his glass on the table and accepted the offering from Stefan. He took a small sip and sighed in appreciation. "That's some mighty fine whiskey."

Stefan winced slightly. "Bourbon, actually. You can only buy it at the Evan Williams distillery in Kentucky. I try to have a bottle of it on hand any place I know I'm going to be."

Though Major continued to sip from his glass, he remained silent.

"I was speaking with Brendan O'Malley. He's some piece of work. I will get him off your back, Major. You have my word. In fact, I plan on banning him from selling SeaCirque entirely."

"Then what's he doing here?" Gabi blurted out.

Stefan turned to Gabi. "His rep, and your rep, John Clarke invited him. He was simply doing his job, inviting all the advisors in his territory to the event. Just like he invited you, Gabi."

"John is Brendan's rep? But if Connor's agency was one of yours, why—"

Major stiffened at her words, but Stefan's always-in-place smile barely wavered.

"Connor did a strong group business. I found it useful to work with him directly." Stefan turned to Major. "But, of course, that's all conveniently in the past now. Isn't it, Major?"

Major raised his glass to Stefan. "To business," he said holding Stefan's gaze and flinging the rest of the bourbon down his throat. "I appreciate the bourbon, Stefan."

Stefan's eyes narrowed at the implicit dismissal in Major's voice. "Please enjoy dinner," he said to them both before walking away.

Stefan's presence had put an end to their previous conversation, and the two sat quietly for a little while. Gabi broke the silence, her curiosity once again prompting her to speak up. "So, the FBI," she said, letting the last syllable linger.

"You mean, why me?" Major said. She nodded. "Well, I did threaten him, didn't I?"

"Yes, but lots of people threaten other people and don't mean it or act on it."

"Really? You've told someone you're going to kill them before?"

"Well, no. But I've said 'or else.'"

Major chuckled.

"The FBI agent I spoke with," Gabi pressed on. "His name is Agent Jacks. He said your military background makes you a good suspect."

Major's eyebrows rose for a second. "I'm surprised he shared that information with you. They're really not supposed to."

"Well, I can be charming when I want to be," she answered, batting her eyelids at Major. "And they did tell me, so there's no reason you can't add context now, right?"

Major laughed again. "You really are something. They didn't give me many details, but they asked a lot about my experience with plastic explosives. It sounds like that's what was used to separate the rigging Connor was strapped into from the parasail. As ex-military, it was clear the feds assumed I'm an explosives expert."

"Are you?"

"I know a little something," Major answered. The tone of his voice indicated he was not inclined to continue the conversation, so she changed the subject once again.

"Can Stefan really ban Brendan from selling SeaCirque?"

Major's face softened and he sighed. "Yeah, I think so. Brendan is too much of a goon for Stefan to tolerate. He's too over the top, and Stefan knows it's not a good look for the line."

"Brendan and John looked pretty cozy just a few minutes ago. You think John knows what Brendan's up to?"

"I don't know. I really don't know anything about John."

"They're both Irish. I mean, Irish Irish, you know, like from Ireland. Maybe they knew each other from before they came to the States. Oh, that reminds me. Sophia and I saw John and Brendan talking on the *Sea Fantasy*, on the same day Connor died. They were sort of huddled together in the card room. I wonder…"

From behind Major, a hand, attached to the unbelievably long arm of a thin man slinking his way alongside the table, reached for Major's scotch glass and then slowly retracted, glass in hand. Major jumped to the side with such force that if the stool he'd been sitting on hadn't been attached to the floor, it would have gone flying. Gabi lurched backwards at the same time, nearly falling off her stool.

"So sorry to startle, sir, ma'am," said one of the gangliest men she had ever seen. Over six feet in height, the man was mostly long arms and legs. He was decked out in a silver-studded black pleather jumpsuit and a full facemask that made her physically shudder. The mask was a parody of the comedy/tragedy theater arts mask, but instead of the dual smiling and frowning faces, there were two skeletal faces.

One displayed a grimacing smirk, and the other had a gaping mouth, frozen in pain or horror.

Before Major or Gabi could find any words to reply, the man slowly extended his arm again, this time to retrieve Gabi's discarded Bellini. "Have a good evening," he said in what she surmised was his best Lurch imitation.

She watched the man slink along the wall, slowly picking up discarded glasses and beer bottles as he went. When she turned back to Major, she found him still standing, his hand pressed to his chest.

"Are you okay? Sit down. That was… Honestly, I don't know what that was, but it was definitely disturbing."

Major remained silent, hand still pressed to his chest, which was visibly rising and falling as he tried to catch his breath.

"He scared me, that's for sure," she said, trying to steady her nerves with words, but a nervous laugh bubbled up. Though she clamped a hand over her mouth to still the laughter, she couldn't hold it back. Major stared blankly at her for a second, and then as he watched Gabi succumb to her laughter, he started chuckling as well.

"I don't think I've been that startled in a mighty long time," Major proclaimed, his southern twang more pronounced.

"That was like in a horror movie, when the monster suddenly jumps out from behind the bushes and everyone in the theater jumps." Gabi was still laughing, and she had to wipe tears from her eyes.

"Someone's coming," Major said.

Thinking he was imitating a horror film, she laughed harder. But when Major didn't join in, Gabi turned to look behind her.

John Clarke was headed their way with three beers clasped between his hands.

"Hi Gabi," he said as he approached. "I saw you on the elevator earlier, but I had to run and meet someone so couldn't stop to say hi."

As he reached them, he held his arms out for her to take one of the beers. Once she did, he offered one to Major.

Smiling at them both, John lifted his beer. "To the Hotel de Cirque and all the bookings she is goin' to bring us. *Sláinte*."

Neither Gabi nor Major responded immediately, but John's smile and enthusiasm seemed genuine, so Gabi suddenly felt bad for leaving him hanging. She tapped her beer against his. Major followed suit.

If John picked up on the distrust Gabi and Major were feeling, he showed nothing of it. "I'm sorry we're not goin' to be working together, Major. Jill always has such nice things to say about you."

John's light brogue gave his words a sing-song quality. "Sometimes I think if she weren't married, and you, yourself not married, she'd be makin' a play for you." His easy banter elicited smiles from Gabi and Major. "Ah, but you're getting to work with the best of us. And I've still got the lovely Gabi." John reached out and gave Gabi a brief one-armed hug.

Gabi couldn't help it. John's cheer and friendly manner worked their way through the suspicion she was feeling, melting it away.

A bell tinkled over the PA system, indicating dinner was ready to be served. Gabi, Major, and John joined the throng threading its way up the half staircase and into the banquet room.

Dinner was a three-hour affair with four courses and too many speeches. Most advisors were free to seat themselves wherever they wanted. But as a new member of Stefan's hand-selected advisors, Major was assigned to Stefan's table.

So, Gabi grabbed a seat near the back of the room, while Major and John headed to the front.

Gabi spent most of the dinner talking with Alicia Jackson, an advisor from Virginia who concentrated much of her business on religious group travel. By the time the food had been eaten and the speeches endured, Gabi had a list of religious cruise ideas to pitch to Elaine.

She met up with Major again as everyone filed out after dinner.

"How was your dinner?" Gabi asked Major.

"Pretty good, surprisingly. Two of the other agents who work with Stefan grew up south of the Mason-Dixon, so we spent at least half of dinner swapping tales of boyhood mischief."

"I always knew that accent of yours wasn't from growing up in Maryland."

"No ma'am. Born and raised in Georgia. I moved north when I joined the Air Force."

"How was sitting with Stefan?"

"You know, it wasn't half bad. Most of the time he was busy with all them speeches of his, but the weirdest thing about being at his table? Stefan actually serves the food himself."

"Um, that seems very un-Stefan-like." Gabi couldn't even begin to imagine Stefan serving food. He was always so proper and formal. Besides, who ever heard of an executive serving food at a fancy dinner?

"I asked one of the other agents about it, and he said Stefan always treats his crew like royalty."

"Maybe it's actually a good thing that Stefan's taken you into his group. Seems like maybe he does want to make amends for the whole Connor thing."

"Yeah, well, I don't know if I'd go that far." Major scowled.

They lingered for all of two minutes amid the throngs waiting for the elevators before realizing they'd make better time on the stairs. Although Major looked tired to Gabi, he insisted he was up for the climb to his sixth-floor room. She figured she could handle six flights as well, but after that, she was definitely grabbing an elevator for the remaining eight floors to her room.

Both began the climb with vigor, but by only the third floor, both were out of breath. Gabi blamed the extra fifteen pounds she was always forgetting to lose. At first, she assumed Major's difficulty was due to his obvious fatigue but gave herself a mental kick when she remembered that he'd had bypass surgery a few years prior. Passing the fourth floor, Major slowed even more. His breath was ragged, and he rubbed his chest.

"Are you okay?" she asked. They had paused at the halfway landing beneath the fifth floor. "You look pale. Maybe we should take the elevator from here."

Major swayed for a moment then sat down heavily on a step and coughed. "I need my pill," he said and fished in his shirt pocket for a small plastic bag with green and orange capsules in it. Pulling one out, he placed it under his tongue, and then they both waited silently for the drug to take effect.

"I'm tired, Gabi. I used to love my job, but now, every day I wake up afraid to find out that yet another client has broken ranks. I'm afraid Brendan will call again. Afraid he'll do something to Violet. And I'm not the kind of man who is used to being afraid."

She sat next to him and placed her hand on his forearm. "You heard Stefan. He's going to ban Brendan from selling. You'll get all your old clients back, and you won't have to worry about threats anymore."

"And what if Brendan blames me for that? What if he decides to retaliate?"

Gabi had no immediate answer, so Major continued. "No. It's not worth it. Not at my age. That's why coming here was kind of moot. I'm retiring, Gabi."

"What?" Her voice rose. "But you shouldn't have to. That's not fair. There must be another option."

"It's not only all of this. There's also me being the number-one suspect in Connor's death. Plus, I know I'm pretty good to look at…" He tried for levity, but it fell flat when she didn't even smile. "But my ticker isn't what it once was. I'm not up for a long, drawn-out fight. I want to retire in peace and enjoy the rest of my life with Violet. We've even been talking about buying an RV and traveling around the country a bit."

"An RV? But…" Gabi didn't know what to say. She didn't like it. Didn't like that first Connor and now Brendan had pushed him to the edge. She was old enough to know life wasn't fair, but this was ridiculous. Still, she understood that if his heart really was giving him problems, maybe retirement was what he needed. "I'll miss you," she finally said.

His breathing more even, Major pulled himself up by holding on to the staircase handrail.

"We'll always have the Hotel de Cirque." He forced a grin and held his hand out to her to help her up. "Hey, just because I'm retired doesn't mean we can't e-mail anymore. Maybe we'll even come RV-ing up your way."

Gabi remained quiet as they approached the sixth floor. Both of them were breathing heavily again, and Major had started coughing. Though he had briefly lost his balance again, he refused to stop until they reached the sixth floor.

"I've got that," she said, pushing on the heavy door that led to the hallway.

"I'm good from here," Major said, though his breath was still labored. "The elevators are that way."

"Okay, thanks. Well, good night, I guess. I'll see you at breakfast, right?"

"I'll be there," he said reassuringly.

He does look a bit better, she thought. Color was returning to his face, his breathing had slowed, and he hadn't coughed since going through the door.

"We'll tour the port and amusement park together. Then we'll head out to my place for a nice home-cooked meal." Major paused, as if considering his words. "There's something more I haven't told you, and I know you'll want to hear it. Even though I'm retiring, I haven't given up completely on getting some kind of restitution from SeaCirque. I've been in touch with a lawyer."

Her curiosity poked its way through the worry and sadness she was feeling. "A lawyer?"

Major laughed at her predictable response. "It can wait until tomorrow." He chuckled at her obvious disappointment. "Good night, Gabi. See you in the a.m."

"Good night, Major." On impulse, she reached up on her toes and kissed him on the cheek. "Get a good night's rest."

She turned and headed towards the elevators.

"And Gabi," Major called after her. "Be careful, you hear?"

"Yes, sir, Major, sir," she said, turning to give him a small salute.

8

———

GABI FELT MORE excited than she'd ever felt before. She'd figured it out and couldn't wait to tell her dad. Too impatient to wait for the elevator, she raced up three flights of stairs to the cancer ward.

At the heavy door, she had to stop and push as hard as she could. Once through, she felt herself running against a heavy current. Her legs pumped furiously, but her forward movement was sluggish and slow. Her strained momentum halted completely as she collided with a man carrying bed sheets, which made no sense. The sheets were never changed during visiting hours. Her nose wrinkled as she pushed past him. The sheets smelled bad.

"Daddy, I figured it out!" she exclaimed then stopped short. Daddy wasn't there, and the bed was empty and stripped bare.

Gabi woke abruptly, her heart pounding, sweat sticky on her neck. Disoriented by the vividness of the dream, the unfamiliar surroundings of the hotel room sent her into a near panic. She fumbled with the blanket, struggling to get out of bed.

Finally free of entanglement, she lunged out of bed and rapped her knee against a wooden chair. The sharp pain jolted her into full awareness.

"Get ahold of yourself, Gabi," she growled, cupping her knee as she collapsed back on the bed. It was only a dream, but the fact that it was so much like the dream she'd had the night Connor died bothered her. Clearly, all the talk about Connor and death threats had triggered something in her mind. Whenever she thought too much about death, she almost always dreamed of her dad.

A sudden knock on the room door startled her. *Am I late for breakfast?* she wondered. She glanced at the bedside clock radio as she hurried to the door. The numbers stopped her short. It wasn't even 7:00 yet. It was too early for Major to be collecting her for breakfast.

"Yes," she called through the door. She lifted her eye to the peephole. Two men in dark suits stood outside. One of the men held a badge up to the peephole. He was middle-aged, probably a good 10 years older than her, a bit squat but powerful looking, like he might have been a wrestler in his younger days.

"Baltimore P.D. We're looking for Miss Gabriella Feraru."

Her first thoughts were of Aunt Maggie until common sense prevailed. Policemen didn't come to a person's hotel door to tell them a family member had died from cancer—especially not in another state.

"Yes, that's me. Can you wait a moment while I put something on?"

She grabbed the crumpled T-shirt she'd worn on the drive down to Baltimore off the floor and pulled it over her green camisole. It didn't match her plaid sleep boxers, but she doubted the police officers would care. She opened the door.

"I'm Gabi Feraru. How can I help you, Detective?"

The lead detective nodded at the inside of her room, and

she stepped aside to let them in. Hurriedly, she moved her clothes from the night before off the desk chair.

"Miss Feraru, I'm Detective Gomez. This is Detective Gilbert. It's our understanding that you spent last night with a Mr. George Thomas."

"Spent the night," Gabi sputtered. "No! I mean, we saw each other yesterday evening, but we did not spend the night together. He's married!" Her voice nearly rose to a squeak on her last word. "Why are you even asking me this?"

Detective Gilbert raised his hand. "I'm sorry. Detective Gomez didn't mean to imply anything untoward, Miss Feraru," he said. He was younger than his partner, with reddish-blond hair and a smattering of freckles that would probably always make him seem youthful, no matter what his age.

"Why are you here? Is Major okay? Is he in trouble? Did something happen?"

"Mr. Thomas was found earlier this morning in the hotel lobby," Detective Gomez replied, whipping out a small notebook from the inside of his suit jacket.

"Found doing what?" She asked, confused.

"I'm sorry to tell you this, Miss Feraru, but Mr. Thomas was found unresponsive. He was pronounced dead on the scene."

Her legs buckled, and she fell backwards onto the edge of the bed.

"We have a few questions we'd like to get answers to," Detective Gomez added.

"Dead? No, that's... That can't... Oh Major." Gabi hugged herself and tears slid down her cheeks.

The younger detective stepped into the bathroom and returned with a tissue box.

"His heart was giving him a little trouble last night, but I didn't think it was really that bad. He was talking about retiring. Oh no! Who's going to tell Violet?"

"We'll take care of that, ma'am. You said he was having heart trouble?" Detective Gilbert prompted her.

"Yes, after dinner. There were so many people waiting to take the elevators, so we decided to take the stairs. But Major ended up having a hard time. He was having trouble breathing and was coughing. We had to stop halfway so he could take a pill and sit and rest."

"And about what time was that?"

Gabi thought for a moment. "About 9:45 maybe. But he was better after that. He'd stopped coughing. His breathing seemed more normal. Was it a heart attack?"

"We don't know yet, but it seems likely. He was a 74-year-old man with a history of cardiovascular problems. Heart attacks happen."

She was stung by the indifference in Detective Gomez's voice.

"Miss Feraru." Detective Gilbert shot his partner a dark look. "Do you happen to know why Mr. Thomas would have been downstairs in the lobby around 5:00 in the morning?"

"No, I don't think so." She racked her brain for any reason Major might have been up and about at that time. "Maybe he couldn't sleep? I know he liked to walk to stay in shape. Could he have been going for a walk?"

"At 5:00 in the morning?" Detective Gomez couldn't hide the sarcasm in his voice.

"Lots of people get up early to go jogging or for a walk. Why not Major?" She asked.

"Gomez, why don't you go back down and check on the progress of the scene investigation." The squat detective gave his partner a quick, angry look before stomping away. "Sorry about him. He doesn't like getting up early, and the coffee shop next door isn't open yet."

Major's dead, and they're upset the coffee shop isn't open, Gabi thought. *Next he'll probably want to know where the nearest donut shop is.* She flinched at her own thoughts. Her dad had been a cop, so she hated it when people made donut jokes.

"Detective Gilbert, there's a man here named Brendan O'Malley. He's another travel advisor, or sort of, anyway. The thing is, he's been threatening Major for the past couple weeks. You should really talk to him."

Detective Gilbert looked at his notepad. "Yes, ma'am, we've already got him on our list of people to speak with. Stefan Davidson was also quick to mention Mr. O'Malley."

"Oh? Was Stefan the one who found Major?"

"No, that would be a John Clarke. But Mr. Clarke called Mr. Davidson after alerting the hotel staff."

"John! Did he say why *he* was in the lobby at 5:00 in the morning?"

"Mr. Clarke found Mr. Thomas at 5:30 this morning as he was heading out to jog. Based on body temperature, the on-scene coroner estimates he died a little before he was found. Please keep in mind, Miss Feraru, we do not suspect foul play here. We're simply trying to tie up loose ends."

"But what if Major was meeting with Brendan and Brendan did something to bring on the heart attack? Maybe he threatened him again or scared him—something like that? Aren't there any security cameras in the hotel that would show what Major was doing there and if somebody did something to him?" Gabi's voice got gradually louder as she spoke.

"Whoa, slow down, Miss Feraru. Of course, anything is possible. The security cameras in the hotel lobby aren't in working order yet. But please keep in mind, in most cases, when an older person with a heart condition dies, they died of a heart attack."

Gabi slowly flipped through the photo album. It had been years since she'd picked it up. The album was full of pictures of her dad. Aunt Maggie had made it for her dad's funeral so people could remember him as he'd been before he got sick. She paused at her favorite photo. In it, she and her dad, dressed identically as Sherlock Holmes, posed dramatically. Each clenched a pipe in their teeth, and she held a magnifying glass above her dad's shoe while he held his above her head. The photo had been taken two years before he died, on the last Halloween before he got sick. She had been ten years old.

She traced her dad's image with her finger.

"Gabi?"

She looked up from the chair she sat in, next to her aunt's bed. "Hi Aunt Maggie. How are you feeling?"

Aunt Maggie held out her hand, inviting Gabi to come closer. "A better question is how are you feeling? It's only been two days since your friend died. How are you doing?"

"I still don't really believe it. It feels so unreal." She paused a moment, twirling her ponytail with her right hand. "Aunt Maggie, I'm so sorry about Friday."

"Shh, it's okay. What are you looking at?" Aunt Maggie gestured at the photo album Gabi was holding.

"It's the album of Daddy you made."

"Wow, it's been a long time since I've seen that."

She moved to sit on the edge of her aunt's bed, and together, they flipped through the pages. They stopped at the photo of Gabi and her dad.

"You really were two peas in a pod. He adored you, and you adored him right back. You wanted to be just like him when you grew up."

"I still miss him, even though sometimes, I'm not sure I

even remember him. It's not fair that he got sick. It's not fair that you're sick. It's not fair that Major died. It's all not fair." Tears streamed down her cheeks.

"Oh Gabi, come here."

Gabi leaned forward, laying her head softly on her aunt's chest. Her aunt stroked her hair until she was too weak to lift her arm anymore.

"Life isn't fair, Gabi. You know that. There's nothing we can do except accept it."

"I don't want to. I don't want you to die." Tears streamed down her cheeks, soaking her aunt's blanket.

"It doesn't matter what you or I want, sweetheart. We both know I'm dying."

She looked at her aunt. Sunlight streamed in from the window on their right, making the too-thin skin on her aunt's arms and hands nearly translucent. Dark-blue veins stood out like tiny mountain ranges along her arms. She couldn't bring herself to say the words.

"Well, I don't accept Major's death," she said instead.

"He's dead," her aunt replied, brows drawn together in confusion.

Gabi sighed in frustration. "I mean, I don't accept that his death was natural or that the feds are probably going to pin Connor's death on him, especially since he can't defend himself now."

"Stop and think for a second, okay?" Aunt Maggie spoke softly and with an intensity that made it clear to Gabi that she wanted her to listen. "I know Major was your friend, but there's nothing you can do about it now. Trying to get justice for him is all well and good, but it won't change what happened to him. It won't bring him back. It won't make it hurt any less for you. It. Won't. Change. Anything."

"I know, but if I can prove that Major didn't…"

"Gabi, I love you, but you are not a detective. Leave the

detecting to the FBI. Maybe Major did kill that man. And if he didn't, then someone out there is a killer, and I don't want you getting hurt."

She didn't answer her aunt, but the thoughts didn't stop swirling in her head. Yeah, life wasn't fair, but she wasn't ready to lie down belly up and surrender yet.

9

———————

Gabi flinched each time the guns discharged, firing blanks into the air in honor of a fallen soldier. Five rows of military men, mostly Air Force, and at least half retired, stood at attention and saluted. A lone bugler began to blow "Taps" into the eerie stillness that followed the gun salute, and Gabi and Alina clenched each other's hand as they both fought back tears. Three honor guard soldiers, stiff in their royal blue uniforms, stepped forward to remove and fold the flag that lay on Major's casket. On the lead soldier's first step toward Violet with flag in hand, an involuntary sob wrenched its way from inside her. The soldier's steps faltered for only a second. Because Violet was too distraught to take the flag from the young man's hands, the woman sitting next to her accepted it on her behalf. The soldier pivoted and returned to stand with the rest of the honor guard.

In the wings, cemetery staff waited for the mourners to move away so they could begin the dirty task of covering up the coffin.

As Gabi and her sister joined the line of people filing

away from the grave, she spotted John Clarke standing off to the side. Before she had gotten past the last row of chairs, John had already walked to the narrow road that ran through the cemetery. By the time she was finally able to maneuver her way around the people in front of her, leaving her sister behind, John had already slipped into a black sedan and was driving away. How strange that John was at Major's funeral, especially since they'd hardly known each other. Had he been there to represent SeaCirque? If so, why had he left before even paying his condolences to Violet?

Four hours later, she and her sister were among a few people left at Violet's house. The others were either family or a handful of Major's closest friends, all Air Force veterans. They hadn't intended to linger so long, but Violet had asked Gabi to stay so they could talk.

The house Major had shared with Violet was small. It had two bedrooms, with one doing double duty as a guest room and an agency office. A small veranda wrapped around the front of the house, tapering off on both sides as it reached the back. Potted plants hung from the eaves, and a white-washed swinging bench, big enough for two, was angled in one corner.

Gabi had gone outside onto the veranda to get some air, when Violet came out as well. She had long since changed out of the stiff, black skirt suit she'd worn to the funeral and into a simple black cotton dress. She sat down on the bench and patted the spot next to her. Gabi's throat closed at the gesture. She could easily picture Violet and Major sharing the seat on a cool evening, watching the sunset together—something they'd never get to do again.

Gabi swallowed the lump in her throat. "Maybe I should stand?"

Violet looked down at the bench, her eyes red-rimmed.

"George would've told you to stop being such a ninny and sit."

They sat without talking. Through the window, Gabi could see Alina chatting with Violet's sister in the kitchen. As the silence stretched on, she wondered if Violet was waiting for her to speak first.

"Um…"

"Gabi, I wanted to talk to you about the night George died."

Gabi froze. *Did Violet blame her for Major's death?* The thought had haunted her every day since he'd died. If they had taken the elevator instead of the stairs, or if she'd insisted he rest longer, would Major still be alive?

"The police said it was probably a heart attack." Gabi tensed, waiting for Violet's recrimination.

"Well, I don't believe that. I've requested an autopsy."

Gabi turned her head sharply to look at Violet.

"I know he has a heart condition. Of course I know. Wasn't I the one sitting in the waiting room when he had his bypass surgery? But that was almost three years ago. We take long walks every day. We have stairs in the house."

Gabi noticed Violet spoke about Major in the present tense, and she felt her throat tighten again.

"George mows the lawn. His heart might not be the strongest in the world, but it's…" She paused, perhaps finally hearing herself speaking as if her husband were still alive. "It wasn't weak enough to have suffered another heart attack."

Gabi couldn't help but remember how Major had clutched at his heart when that masked circus guy had scared them and how ashen he'd looked when they'd had to stop to rest on the stairs. But she kept those memories to herself. Violet didn't need to hear them.

"The police wouldn't answer any of my questions, so

you're all I've got." Violet stopped speaking for a moment and swallowed hard. "Was Brendan there?"

Gabi exhaled in a rush of air she hadn't realized she'd been holding. "Yes."

Violet blanched and her eyes teared up, but she nodded. "Is there any way he could have done this?"

It was the same question Gabi had asked the police that morning and the same question she'd thought about whenever she wasn't blaming herself for Major's death.

She grabbed a fistful of hair and tugged. "I don't know. I asked the cops the same thing, and they said they'd look into it. I can tell you I never saw Major and Brendan come into contact with each other at the event. But, Violet, I don't know what Major was doing in the lobby at 5:00 in the morning. Do you?"

"No, I don't." She shook her head. She stared, unseeing, into the night. "The thing is, George had been acting weird the past few days. I know that sounds vague, but he'd been so depressed since Brendan started making those horrible calls about two weeks ago. And then suddenly, about three days before he went to meet you in Baltimore, his attitude changed. Suddenly he was smiling and whistling to himself, but when I asked him about it, he wouldn't say."

"Major told me he was retiring," Gabi said. "Could it have been that?"

"He told me that too. It was around the same time he stopped moping around, in fact. I was surprised. He loves… loved being a travel agent. But I don't think that was it. Yes, he seemed content with his decision to retire, but the strange, overly happy demeanor? It was almost like…" Violet paused, as if to put her thoughts into words. "Well, the way he was acting, it was like the cat that swallowed the canary. There was something he wasn't telling me. I know it."

"The last time I saw Major"—Gabi forced herself past the

pain of the memory—"he told me that even though he was retiring, he hadn't given up completely. That he'd even been in touch with a lawyer. But he wouldn't tell me more. Did he ever say anything about that to you? Do you know what lawyer he was talking about?"

Alina chose that moment to join the two of them outside, and the squeaking of the screen door stopped the conversation for a brief moment. She carried two glasses of wine in her hands and a bottle of water squeezed against her side. She handed one of the glasses to Gabi.

"Your sister said you'd prefer this," Alina said, handing the bottle of water to Violet.

Violet's voice was soft, and Gabi could hear the hurt in it when Violet again spoke. "I didn't know he'd called a lawyer. He never said anything to me."

"Do you know what he might have been talking to a lawyer about?"

"All I know is George had been trying to confirm that Connor was stealing his clients for the past three years. But he had never been able to prove anything. Everyone who left George to book with Connor said it was because they knew George wasn't well. They said they liked him, but they were afraid he'd end up being too ill to take care of them. No matter what he said to them, they wouldn't listen. And no matter what he said to SeaCirque, they said Connor hadn't done anything wrong."

"What did Major think Connor was doing? Was he rebating?" At Violet's blank look, Gabi rephrased her question. "Did he think Connor was giving a portion of his commission away to clients in order to lower their fares? That's how most advisors steal other people's clients, and it's totally against the rules of most cruise lines."

"That sounds familiar, I think. But he couldn't prove anything. I remember him telling me that SeaCirque had looked into it and found that all his old clients had paid full price for their cruises."

"But Major didn't believe it?" Alina spoke up, caught up in the conversation.

"No. He was convinced Connor told everyone to lie about what they paid. But it was more than that. He was always telling me something was off at SeaCirque. That something wasn't quite right, but he could never put his finger on what he thought was wrong. I honestly believe the people at SeaCirque tried to take his complaint seriously at first, but after their investigation turned up nothing and George kept on about something being wrong, well, I think they wrote him off as a paranoid old man. That Stefan Davidson even called him a crazy old man when we were on the *Sea Fantasy*. That's what set George off the day he hit Connor."

"What a jerk!" Alina said. "No wonder Major lost his temper."

Gabi pushed her hair back. A breeze was kicking up, blowing strands of hair into her face. Instinctively, she reached for her jeans pocket to grab a ponytail holder she always kept with her, only to remember she'd put on a skirt for the funeral. In the distance, she could see street debris swirl gently in unseen currents.

"Do you think Major was paranoid?"

Violet looked at Gabi, her eyes dark pools of grief that absorbed what little light was left in the sky. "George had good instincts. If he thought something was wrong, then something was wrong. And Brendan's threats? To me, the fact that he was making them says something bigger is going on."

"And when you figure in Connor's murder… Yeah, something doesn't add up," Gabi said.

"Unless you believe that George murdered Connor," Violet nearly spat the words.

Gabi covered Violet's hand with her own. "I don't believe for a second that Major killed Connor."

"Neither do I," Alina added.

"And if the FBI give it some thought, I'm sure they'll come to the same conclusion," Gabi said.

Violet's eyes teared up again. "Oh Gabi, I don't think they're going to give it any more thought. George is dead. He can't defend himself anymore. They can say whatever they want, so the case will be closed. Please, you have to help me. Don't let them pin this on George." She began sobbing.

Gabi put an arm around Violet, holding her. "Violet, I don't know what I can do." She looked at her sister, who shook her head at her.

"Violet, we both loved Major, but Gabi's a travel agent, not a cop," Alina said. "You'd be better off hiring a private investigator. We'd both be happy to help pay for one if you need."

"No, no. I don't think I could trust someone who didn't know Major. Please, Gabi, I don't know who else to ask."

Gabi tried to calm Violet, all the while avoiding the are-you-nuts glares her sister was aiming at her. Inside, she felt anything but calm. She knew Major hadn't killed Connor. And she truly believed Major hadn't died from a heart attack. That meant someone had committed murder—twice.

"Do you know how crazy that sounds?" Sophia asked Gabi. It was the day after the funeral and Gabi could feel the beginnings of a headache forming, the result of the long drive back to NJ and a restless night of sleep.

Early morning sunlight streamed in through Best in Travel's storefront window, the rays broken apart by vacation posters taped to the glass.

"What do you think I've been trying to tell her since yesterday?" Alina said.

Gabi looked at her best friend and her sister and sighed. Sophia was touching up a chip on a manicured finger, while Alina pulled out the bagels and tub of cream cheese she'd brought with her after dropping the kids off at school. So much for getting any work done.

"Yes, I know it's crazy," she said, grabbing an egg bagel from the paper plate her sister had piled them on. "I don't know what Violet expects me to do, but I couldn't say no."

"Yes, you could have," Sophia and Alina said in unison.

"Besides, you don't know anything for sure. Where do you even start?" This time, Sophia was the lucky recipient of Alina's glare.

"Don't you dare encourage her," her sister said.

"Sure, I do. First, I know Connor was murdered." Gabi counted off the points on her fingers. "Second, I know it wasn't Major."

"Gabi-doll," Sophia cut her off gently. "How do you know it wasn't Major?

Gabi slammed her bagel down on the desk, scaring Bugsy, who had crept under her desk to escape the smell of Sophia's nail polish. He sprang up, hissed at her, and ran to hide behind the oversized fern in one of the office's back corners.

"Do you really think Major killed Connor?" She asked the two women, looking each in the face, one at a time. "Well, do you?"

"I'm with Gabi on this one thing," Alina said. "We got to know Major pretty well last year during the fam in Jamaica. I don't believe he was capable of murder."

"Fine. All I'm saying is we don't really know for sure though, do we," Sophia said.

"Yes, we do." Gabi felt restless. Neither she nor Sophia

had any client meetings or phone calls scheduled before noon, and a walk-in on a Wednesday morning was unlikely. Finishing up the first half of her bagel and suddenly feeling the need to move, she decided now would be as good a time as any to switch out the Mexican Riviera poster in the window for a made-to-order "Close to Home, but Far, Far Away" poster she'd created to highlight family vacation options along the East Coast.

Sophia stood as well, blowing on her fingertip and watched as Gabi began to peel the tape off the poster. "Fine, I don't really believe Major killed Connor either. But I'm not convinced Major was murdered. He did have a heart problem."

"You did say you were scared for him on the stairs," Alina reminded Gabi.

"I don't think it's such a leap of faith to say that his heart finally gave up," Sophia concluded the thought.

Gabi paused halfway through rolling the poster up. Bugsy darted out from behind the fern to bat at a stray piece of tape that had floated to the floor. Her shoulders slumped, and she handed the partially rolled poster to her sister. "I know."

She gazed out the window through the open space, waiting to be covered by the new poster. Across the street, she watched as several bouquets of flowers were loaded into Roses Are Red's delivery truck. "I don't know which is worse —thinking someone may have killed Major, or that he died of a heart attack I might have helped contribute to."

"Oh Gabs." Sophia placed a hand on Gabi's shoulder. "You can't think like that. It's not your fault."

Gabi pulled away from Sophia, dropping the tape dispenser on the floor as she did so. "If Major's death wasn't murder, then how isn't it my fault? I suggested the stairs," she said, her voice getting louder as she continued. "I kept pushing him for information. I wanted to know what was going on. He was already under a lot of stress, and all I did was add to it."

"Your questions weren't what was stressing Major out," Alina said, stepping forward. "Connor caused him stress when he stole clients. SeaCirque caused him stress when they dismissed him as paranoid. The FBI caused him stress when they let him know he was their prime suspect in Connor's death. Brendan caused him stress with all his threats. You're right, Major was under a lot of stress, but none of it came from you."

"But—"

"No buts, Gabs." It was Sophia's turn again. "You. Didn't. Kill. Major."

Gabi slowly turned around to face her sister and best friend. Both stood facing her, hands on their hips with matching enough-is-enough looks on their faces. She let their words sink in, and as she did, something her sister had said clicked in her mind.

Angling her head to the side, she chewed on the thought for a moment and then slowly spoke. "If the FBI believed Major killed Connor, wouldn't they have told Connor's family? And wouldn't his family then have believed Major killed Connor?"

Sophia and Alina looked blankly back at Gabi, not following her.

"Why was Brendan calling Major to threaten him about his business? Why was he trying to stop him from taking his clients back? Why wasn't he calling Major, upset that he'd killed his brother-in-law? Why was it 'keep out of Connor's business' and not 'if I find out you killed my brother-in-law, I'm going to kill you'? It's like he knew Major didn't kill Connor."

"Are you saying Brendan killed Connor?" Sophia asked.

Gabi paused, trying to let the ideas racing through her mind coalesce. Idly, she picked up the new poster and unrolled it. She picked up the tape dispenser from the floor and handed it to Alina before flattening the poster against the window.

"Maybe Brendan *did* kill Connor. And maybe he killed Major to keep him from finding that out and, more importantly, from finding out why." Gabi wiggled her fingers at Alina to ask for tape.

"That's complete speculation. You can't possibly know that for sure," Alina said, handing Gabi three long pieces of tape.

"And if it is true," Sophia added, "then Brendan is a dangerous man and you need to stay out of it. Let the FBI and the police handle this."

Gabi finished taping the bottom corners and darted outside before Sophia could continue. While the traffic light at the corner was red, she ran into the street and turned to inspect the poster to make sure it wasn't crooked.

"The Baltimore police think it's a heart attack. Other than waiting on the autopsy that Violet requested, they've basically stopped investigating," Gabi said, continuing their conversation as she reentered the office. "That's why Violet asked for my help. How can I say no?"

"Your help? What kind of help can you give Violet? You're a travel agent. Sorry, advisor," Alina added after Gabi's eyebrows drew together in a you-know-better look.

"You track down late payments, not murderers," Sophia added.

"Truthfully, I don't know what Violet expects me to do. I don't know what I *can* do, but I feel like I've got to do something. I can't turn my back on her, and I can't ignore what's inside here." Gabi pressed her hands against her chest. "I can't explain it, but something is telling me I've got to make this right."

"Gabi, no matter what you do, it won't bring—" Alina was prevented from finishing her sentence when the phone on Gabi's desk rang.

"Don't bother holding that thought," Gabi said, turning her back on her sister and picking up the phone.

10

———————

"Take care of yourself and let me know when the baby is born. Bye, Jill." Gabi hung up the phone and looked at the phone numbers she'd jotted down on the pad in front of her. Though Jill had called to say good-bye before going on maternity leave for the next three months, they had also gotten around to talking about Major. Realizing what a great opportunity it was, Gabi had found herself asking Jill for information about the clients Connor had poached from Major. It didn't take too long before she had cajoled Jill into giving her the names and numbers of the group leaders of two of the largest bookings Connor had taken.

She peeked at Sophia's desk. It was still empty. For much of Gabi's conversation with Jill, Sophia and Alina had been blatantly eavesdropping. But then Sophia had gotten a call and Alina had left for her class at the gym. Sofia left shortly thereafter.

Gabi knew they didn't want her getting involved in anything, but she couldn't let it go, not yet anyway. Before she lost her nerve, she picked up the phone and dialed the first number in her notes. The phone rang three times before voicemail picked up. Gabi panicked when she realized she didn't know what to say and hung up.

Breathe, she told herself. She needed a plan and a reason for calling. She couldn't call a stranger and say, *"Hi there, are you lying about why you left Major for Connor and about how much you paid for the cruises you booked through him?"*

She dialed the first number again. This time, a man picked up after two rings.

"Hello, Mr. Moore? My name is Gabi Feraru. I'm a travel advisor and was a friend of Major Thomas."

"I was so sorry to hear about Major. What can I do for you Miss Feraru?"

"I hope I'm not being too forward, but I know that you were a client of both Major and Connor Foley, and now that they're both…" she paused, not sure exactly how to put it. "Um, now that both are no longer with us"—she winced at her bad choice of words but pushed on—"I thought perhaps you might need some help with your SeaCirque bookings."

The line was silent for a moment, and then Mr. Moore replied, his voice noticeably cold. "You say you were a friend of Major?"

"Yes, I was." Gabi hoped this would help her get the information she needed.

"Your friend is barely in the ground, and you're calling me about business? I wouldn't call that a friend, more like a vulture. You are no different than that Irish man who called me."

"Brendan called you? That figures," Gabi spoke more to herself than Mr. Moore.

"I will tell you the same thing I told him. I don't need anything from you," he said and hung up.

Well, that didn't go very well, she thought. In fact, she didn't get a single piece of information from him. She tried calling him back, but the phone just rang, not even going to voicemail.

Stung by how badly the first call went, Gabi waited an hour before trying the second number. A man picked up on the first ring.

"*Necesidades especiales de los niños,*" a man said.

"Um hello, I'm trying to reach Mr. Rodriguez," she said, hoping the man spoke English.

"I am Mr. Rodriguez."

"Hi, Mr. Rodriguez. My name is Gabriella Feraru, and I was a friend of Major Thomas."

"Aye, Major. I was so sorry to hear of his passing." Mr. Rodriguez spoke with a thick Hispanic accent and softened the j in Major so it sounded like mahor. "I knew he had been sick but did not realize it had gotten so bad."

This time, Gabi decided to skip the pretense. "The truth is, he wasn't that sick. Listen, I know this is going to sound crazy and I know that you don't know me, but as I said, Major was my friend and I don't believe he died of a heart attack. I was with him the day before he died. I was at his funeral. His wife doesn't believe it either."

She paused for a moment, and when Mr. Rodriguez didn't speak, she pushed on. "I believe Major was murdered and that his death was related to Connor Foley's death. I know you were a client of both Major and Connor. I was hoping you might be able to help me find out more about Connor." Her words ended in a rush.

They were met, again, with no response.

"Mr. Rodriguez?"

"*Dios mio.* I am not sure I can help."

"Please, Mr. Rodriguez. If you know anything. I *need* to find out what happened to Major. Can you help me?"

"Miss Feraru, you can meet me somewhere? I cannot talk about this here."

"Well, I'm in New Jersey. Could I call you at a different place?"

"No, I do not want to say anything over the phone. It must be in person."

Gabi quickly thumbed through the old-fashioned date book she still relied on. "Okay, then yes. I can meet you, but not until the weekend. You're in Delaware?"

"*Si*. My office is in Dover. Can you meet me at a place called Fraizer's Restaurant on Loockerman Street? On Saturday, at noon?"

Gabi knew absolutely nothing about Dover, or about Delaware for that matter. She hated driving in unfamiliar cities, but the lure of what Mr. Rodriguez might know was too great to let that stop her. "Okay, Mr. Rodriguez. I'll see you at noon on Saturday."

Gabi's hand was trembling as she hung up the phone. "Okay," She whispered to herself on a long exhale. She nodded once, then again, then didn't stop nodding. "Okay," she said louder. "I'm actually doing this." She sat up straight and then thumped her fists gently on the desk. "Right, okay."

Gabi looked around the empty office. Two note cards that clients had used as thank-you notes stood propped on the corner of her desk. The bottom right-side corner of the *Pubs of Ireland* poster on the wall behind Sophia's desk was slightly curled. On the desk, Sophia had left a bottle of top-coat nail polish open, and if it wasn't closed soon, Bugsy was probably going to spill it everywhere. A pile of unopened mail lay in Elaine's inbox, and Gabi briefly wondered when or if her boss would be coming by this week.

Slowly, Gabi's head nodding stopped and her spine curled inward again. "Oh boy. What did I just do?"

~

"What the hell am I doing here?" Gabi asked herself, not for the first time, as she drove past the same gas station for the third time. She was in Dover and hopelessly lost after her phone's GPS had tried to send her the wrong way on a one-way street. After getting herself turned around, she had smacked the thing in frustration, accidentally sending it tumbling to the passenger-seat floor. Now she couldn't reach it, and she seemed to be driving in circles.

"This was a mistake. Sophia was right," She muttered as she made a left turn and hoped the street would take her in the right direction. Sophia had been royally pissed when she'd learned that Gabi had arranged to meet Mr. Rodriguez, and after Sophia's reaction, Gabi hadn't had the guts to tell her sister. Now that she was actually in Dover, totally out of her element, she was beginning to agree with Sophia.

"I mean, seriously, what do I really think I can do?" she scolded herself. "I'm not a cop." Ahead of her, she could see that the street was coming to a fork with a very busy main road. She hoped that road was Loockerman.

Not for the first time on her drive down to Dover, she contemplated hightailing it back to New Jersey. She could call Mr. Rodriguez and tell him she'd made a mistake and that she was sorry she'd wasted his time. But each time, she'd picture Violet sitting alone on the porch swing. Violet needed answers, and so did Gabi.

"If I can at least find out what Connor was up to and prove that Major wasn't crazy or paranoid, that'd be something." Gabi talked to herself, trying to keep calm as the street she was on neared its end. "Then I'd have something concrete to tell the FBI and they'd have to look into it." She had said much the same to Sophia. Now that she could see Loockerman Street in clear letters on the road ahead of her, she began to believe her own words again.

Gabi lucked out, choosing to go right onto Loockerman

Street. Three blocks later, she spotted Fraizer's Restaurant and pulled into the parking lot. A little belatedly, she wondered how she was supposed to recognize Mr. Rodriguez as she pulled the restaurant's front door open. A rush of ice-cold air-conditioned air met her, a relief from the oppressive July heat wave that had begun two days earlier and stretched across most of the Eastern coastline.

Before she had time to look around, a short, dark-haired man approached her. "Miss Feraru?" he asked.

She nodded.

"I'm Miguel Rodriguez," he said. He was maybe two inches taller than her own five feet four inches and wore jean shorts that reached just below his knees and a rusty orange polo shirt. He was younger than Gabi had expected, probably around her own age, in his mid- to late-thirties.

"It's nice to meet you, Mr. Rodriguez." They shook hands.

"Call me Miguel, *por favor*. I am still too young to be a mister."

It took Gabi a moment to adjust to his accent, which turned young into jung and mister into mee-ster. "Me too," she said. "Please call me Gabi."

The hostess led them to a table at the back of the restaurant, handed them their menus, and left. "How did you know it was me?" Gabi asked. She opened her menu, trying to hide the coldness she felt towards the man. The minute Miguel had introduced himself, she had been surprised by a wave of anger. This man was one of the people who had abandoned Major and then lied about it. For a moment, she forgot why she was there. Instead, she wanted to hold him accountable for having hurt Major.

"I watch for a car with New Jersey license plate. I am glad you drove down. I know it is a long drive and on a very hot day."

"Don't worry about it. That's what A/C is for." Despite her anger, she tried to keep her tone of voice mild, reminding herself she wasn't there to punish him. She was there to help Violet and figure out what had gotten Major killed. She didn't want to upset Miguel before she could get the information she had come for.

"*Si*, that is true, but I am glad you came. I want to help. I really did like Major… I always feel guilty about leaving him for Connor. And now you say Major's death was not heart attack. If that is true, I need to tell someone the truth."

Gabi's anger cooled as Miguel talked. He spoke earnestly, and she couldn't help but believe him. Miguel was not the greedy, penny-pinching ogre Gabi had been expecting. Instead, he seemed like a genuinely nice guy. Even so, she couldn't help but ask, "Then why did you leave Major like that?"

"Do you know what kind of group I bring on the cruises?"

She had to admit she didn't know.

"I bring Hispanic special needs children and their families. Children who have learning disabilities or physical disabilities." As Miguel explained his non-profit to Gabi, she stared at the table, tugging on a strand of hair. "Families whose lives are defined by their children, and families with not a lot of money. Good families, good people. People who need a break. People who deserve a vacation, no?"

She wasn't sure how to respond. This wasn't how she had been expecting the meeting to go. "I," she began, still tugging at the strand of hair she had wrapped around her fingers. "I didn't know that."

The waitress chose that moment to take their orders, seafood gumbo for Miguel and grilled salmon for Gabi.

"Miguel, I'm sorry. I came here angry. I assumed you

were… I don't even know what I assumed, but I was angry that you had—"

"Betrayed Major? *Si, comprendo*. Major was good to us. For three years, he helped us get good rates and worked with SeaCirque to get us special extras, like private movie nights and escorted excursions." Miguel paused, his eyes flickering between her face and a spot behind her head. "But then Major had a heart attack, and Connor Foley reached out to me. And the rate he offered was more than half off what Major had ever gotten for us. With that rate, more families could afford to come."

"How much? It's important. How much was Connor charging you?"

Miguel finally met Gabi's eyes as he told her the price.

"What? No, that's impossible. For a seven-night cruise? In a balcony cabin?" She was shocked. It wasn't just a low price; it was unheard of. Rebating couldn't explain a rate like that. There was no way an advisor could make enough commission to reduce a rate that much. "Are you sure it was per cabin? And not per person? I mean, even per person that's pretty low."

"*Si*, I am sure."

"And SeaCirque was okay with that?" Gabi couldn't wrap her mind around how cheap Connor was selling those cruises for, but Miguel's sudden silence cut into her thoughts. "Miguel?"

"At first, I didn't know anything was wrong. I was surprised, and I wanted to ask Major why he had never been able to get us such a low rate. But Major was in the hospital, and Connor told me I had to decide right away, take it or leave it. So, I took it. How could I not? Many more families would be able to take the vacation they needed. Do you see? So, I say yes.

"But working with Connor was different. He gave us

good price, *si*, but nothing else. No extras, no service, *nada*. He sent us our confirmations, and that was it. If we had a question, he didn't have an answer. He told us to call the cruise line. But the cruise line always said we had to talk to our travel agent. So back and forth we went. And when we did get ahold of Connor, all he ever said was we could never tell anyone at SeaCirque what we paid. That it was something he'd done only for us because he believed in what we were doing. But no one could know about it."

"And you didn't think that was strange?"

"*Si*, strange, but not wrong. Not for the first two years, anyway. But then there was an investigation, and we started getting calls from SeaCirque. Connor said if I told SeaCirque the truth, all the families that had been on cruises would get in trouble. He said they'd be banned from ever cruising again. Maybe they'd even be in trouble with the police. I didn't know what to do, but I knew I could no risk any of our families getting in trouble."

"So you lied." It wasn't a question. It wasn't a condemnation. She understood.

"I lied."

The waitress arrived with their food, and they ate without talking, each preoccupied with their own thoughts. Gabi kept turning the situation over in her mind, trying to look at it from different angles. By charging such a low rate for the cruises, Connor wasn't only eating into any profit he made from his commission. He'd actually have had to pay out of his own pocket to make up the difference. That didn't make sense, no matter how she looked at it. His agency should have been hemorrhaging money.

On the other hand, if he wasn't making up the difference, then SeaCirque was losing money. And that wasn't something any company would willingly do either. Sure, they might offer up one or two free cruises a year to charities or contests, but they wouldn't choose to lose tens of thousands of dollars by giving away dozens of cabins every year. And that was only taking into account Miguel's group. She knew of at least two other groups that Connor must have been doing the same thing for. Why would someone go out of their way to steal clients from another agent, only to lose money on the bookings? It didn't make any sense.

"Miguel, can you tell me more about working with Connor?" Gabi asked as the waitress cleared away their empty plates.

"How do you mean?"

She sighed, tugging once again on a strand of hair. "I don't know exactly. This whole thing doesn't add up. Maybe if I knew more about Connor, I could make sense of it. Was he easy to work with? Did it seem like he knew what he was doing? Did he have any employees or assistants?"

Miguel took his time answering. "No, it was only Connor. And now that I think about it, no, he never seemed to know much about cruises. He never answer any of my questions. He didn't know where the cruises stopped. He didn't know what restaurants were on board. Half the time, I don't think he even knew the name of the ship we were going on. Other than the low price he get us, I did not like working with him."

"Because he didn't know anything?"

"He was… I don't know the word in English. Like the big children on the playground who push small children?"

"A bully?"

"*Si*, a bully. He never asked us what we wanted, where we wanted to go, or what month was good for us. He told us which cruise we would take and how many cabins we had to book to get the special price."

"I don't get it. He didn't leave any of the details up to you?"

"The last time I spoke to Connor, he tell me I had to book twenty-five cabins on an October cruise. When I try to say no, tell him I need more time, tell him that after last year's investigation, I wasn't sure I want to book another cruise, he say he didn't care what I want. I would make booking, or my families would pay the price."

The waitress returned. "Do you want anything else?"

Both opted for iced coffee. Miguel waited for the woman to walk away before he continued. "It was a threat. Plain and simple. That's when I decide this year would be the last year I work with him, no matter what. I am a honest man. When Connor first approached us, I did what I thought was right for our families. But Connor, he was not a good man. I learned too late, and I was scared. For myself and for the families. I didn't know what I could do, but I knew that this year would be the last with him. Even if it meant no more cruises for our families. But then Connor died. And our reservation was canceled."

"Wait, your booking was canceled? By whom?"

"I don't know. I got a voicemail from someone at SeaCirque a few days after Connor died, saying the reservation was canceled but that we could re-book with another agent."

"That doesn't make sense. Did the person leave a name?"

"No, he only said that he was from SeaCirque. He didn't leave a telephone number either, and my phone showed it as a private number."

Gabi shook her head, adding the facts to the list of others that didn't add up.

"Did you try to rebook?"

"No, I thought about calling Major. I knew I was not going to get the same price, but I didn't care. I wanted to go back to how things used to be. But then some Irish man called me to say I have to book with him, and after that, Major died."

"What exactly did he say when he called? Did he tell you his name?" Gabi asked, sipping her coffee.

"He called two weeks ago. He said he was Connor's, how do you say it, brother of law? I don't remember the name. I think it started with a B. He said he was taking over Connor's agency. But it was clear he knew less about cruises than Connor. When I asked him what it would cost us, he said he'd have to get back to us. I told him I planned to re-book with someone else. He got angry and told me I am making a mistake."

"Did you tell him it was Major you were planning on re-booking with?"

"*Si*." Miguel nodded.

"And was that the only time you spoke with Brendan?"

"Ah, Brendan. Yes, that was his name. No, I talked with him two days before you call. He told me Major was dead, and that, like he already said, he was the only one I could do business with. I told him I'd think about it and hung up. Now, I don't know what to do."

Thoughts raced through Gabi's mind as she tried to make sense of everything Miguel had told her. But she couldn't fit the pieces together. Miguel looked at her, waiting for her to guide him.

"I don't know," she had to admit. "I've never heard of anything like this. Clearly whatever Connor was up to wasn't on the up and up. Maybe this year, your group should skip doing a cruise or go with a different cruise line. I'm pretty sure Brendan isn't going to be allowed to take over Connor's business anyway."

"And do I tell SeaCirque what I tell you?"

Gabi tugged on her hair. She didn't know what was going on, but her gut told her something was very wrong. Had someone at SeaCirque authorized the fantastically low fare Miguel's group had gotten, or had Connor really been swallowing such a huge loss for some reason only he knew about? With two people already dead, she wasn't sure who could be trusted.

"No, I don't think you should tell anyone at the cruise line about this yet." Relief showed plain on Miguel's face until Gabi continued. "But I do think the FBI needs to hear it."

Gabi gave Miguel Agent Jacks's telephone number and made him promise her he'd call.

The stifling July heat hit them as they left the restaurant.

"Thank you so much for speaking with me, Miguel. I know you were nervous about it, and even though I still don't fully understand what's going on, I'm sure the information you gave me is important."

"Do you think it will help you find out who killed Major?" he asked her.

"I hope so. I really do," she said, unlocking her car door and sliding into the driver's seat.

"*Buena suerte,*" Miguel responded.

11

———

"GABI, WHAT'S WRONG?" You're white as a ghost." Sophia had just walked into the office but hurried over to Gabi as she sat at her desk, staring at her office phone.

"Listen to this." She pressed speaker phone and dialed voicemail. Sophia sat perched on the edge of the desk. At the prompt, Gabi pressed four for the saved message. A muffled voice came over the speaker.

"This message is for Gabrielle Fereru," the recording began. "Stop what you're doing." The voice stopped abruptly, but the threat in its tone was clear.

"Who is that? They didn't even get your name right!"

Gabi touched Sophia's hand. "Shh, there's more."

"George Thomas didn't stop, and look what happened to him," the voice said.

Sophia gasped.

"You don't want to meet the same fate."

The sentiment was punctuated by the click of the phone call ending. The women looked at each other in shocked silence.

"Oh my God, Gabi. That's serious." Sophia walked back

to the agency's front door and peered out the glass. Seemingly satisfied with whatever she did or didn't see, she turned to face Gabi. "What are you going to do?"

"Why are you whispering?" Gabi asked.

"Gabi!"

"I don't know what I'm going to do. But I'd be willing to bet anything that was Brendan."

"I didn't hear an accent."

"So, he muffled his voice, right? He could have faked an American accent, too. I mean, come on! He's the one who was calling Major with threats. How is this different?"

"Then you need to tell the FBI."

Gabi had never seen her friend so freaked out before.

"But what do I tell them? That an unidentified caller, who I *think* is Brendan O'Malley, told me to back off?" Gabi said. "Either the FBI will think I'm crazy or be pissed that I've been asking questions."

"So what if they're pissed! You've got to tell someone. What if he *did* kill Connor and Major? You could be next!"

"I know! You think I haven't had the same thought? But what am I supposed to do? The feds think Major killed Connor. They won't appreciate me snooping around and trying to prove them wrong. The Baltimore police pretty much think Major's death was natural. And, after what I learned from Miguel, I don't think calling SeaCirque would be such a good idea either."

"Why not?" Sophia demanded. "Call Stefan. Tell him about the phone call. You don't have to tell him about the real reason you met with Miguel. Tell him you offered to help him out with his booking since both of his previous advisors died."

"That sounds so cold when you put it like that."

"Maybe, but I bet Stefan responds to the its-just-the-business-ness of it."

"Fine, I'll call him," Gabi relented just as the door opened.

"Call who about what, dear?" their boss, Elaine, asked.

As usual, Elaine was decked out in a nautically themed outfit with a pair of navy blue slacks, a horizontally striped blue and white short-sleeve blouse, and a short blue scarf tied around her throat.

"Someone left a threatening message for Gabi on our voicemail, and I said she should tell the FBI, but she doesn't want to, so I told her to at least call Stefan Davidson to let him know," Sophia blurted out, her words tumbling together.

"What kind of threatening call, dear?"

Gabi glared at Sophia but played the message for her boss.

"Oh dear. That does sound serious, Gabriella."

Gabi wanted to stick her tongue out at Sophia, who was giving her a see-I-told-you-so look behind Elaine's back.

"I agree with you though. I don't think it would be a good idea to call those FBI men. I doubt they'd like the idea of you mucking about in their investigation. But calling Stefan sounds like a good idea. He's such a smart man. He might be able to give you some advice, and I don't see what harm it could do."

Exasperated by the expectant look on both Sophia's and Elaine's faces, Gabi picked up the phone. "Fine, I'm calling now. Happy?"

She reached Stefan right away. "Hi Stefan, this is Gabi Feraru from Best in Travel in New Jersey."

"What can I do for you, Gabi?" Stefan Davidson's voice over the phone was, like the man himself, polished and cool. Gabi could hear him typing in the background.

"Well, I, um, I recently spoke with Miguel Rodriguez."

"Miguel Rodriguez? That name sounds familiar."

"Yes, he was a long-time client of Major Thomas."

"Ah, yes, the Special Kidz Foundation." Stefan sounded distracted. "Great organization. If I'm remembering correctly, his was one of the groups caught up in Major's allegations against Connor Foley. May I ask why you were speaking with him?"

"Oh, well." Gabi remembered what Sophia had said about his just-business demeanor. "I figured I'd try for his business, especially as I had been friendly with Major. I thought that would give me a good in."

Stefan chuckled. "I like the way you think, Gabi."

Since getting a new customer wasn't the actual reason she had met with Miguel, she quickly moved on. "That's not why I called you though."

"Oh?"

"This morning, I came into the office to find a message on our company voicemail telling me to *stay out of it*," she emphasized the words so Stefan would understand the implied threat in them. "The man said if I don't, I could end up like Major."

There was silence on the other end of the phone.

"Stefan?"

"It was a man. You are sure of that?"

"No, I'm not sure. The voice is muffled, but I think so."

"It's that awful Brendan O'Malley. I'd put money on it."

Gabi was relieved to hear that Stefan also thought the caller was Brendan.

"Listen, Gabi, there's no need to bring the authorities in on this, okay? I think SeaCirque has had enough bad press, what with Mr. Foley's death and all. I'm already working on getting Brendan O'Malley banned from selling our ships, so he shouldn't be a problem for you much longer. But for the time being, maybe you should stay away from any of Connor's or Major's old clients."

"That's probably a good idea. Thanks, Stefan. I appreciate your time," Gabi said.

"So," Sophia prodded Gabi after she hung up.

Gabi briefly recapped her conversation with Stefan for Sophia and Elaine.

"All right, then. Now we can move on and get back to business as usual because you won't be doing anything else stupid. Right?" Sophia said, more stating a fact than asking Gabi for confirmation.

~

Sunday morning Gabi awoke to an aroma she hadn't smelled in weeks. French vanilla coffee. And chocolate?

"*What the heck?*" She jammed her feet into a pair of slippers and nearly slipped as she sprinted out the door and down the stairs. Her aunt—who, for the past five weeks, had barely been able to rouse herself except when it was time for her radiation or chemo treatments—was dancing around the kitchen to Lionel Ritchie's "Dancing on the Ceiling." In the oven, Gabi could clearly see brownies baking.

"Aunt Maggie! What the… Why aren't you in bed?"

"Oh, Gabi, sweetheart. I don't know. Isn't it wonderful? I woke up to go the bathroom and realized I've got energy. I can't remember the last time I woke up feeling so good. So, I figured I'd do something with myself. I mean, when was the last time I made you brownies?"

"I don't know… A few years, I guess," Gabi replied.

"It was six years ago, actually. Right after that Derek guy broke up with you because you called him out for being rude to the waitstaff every time you went out to dinner."

"Oh, wow, that might actually be right. You remember that?"

"I've been remembering all kinds of things since I woke

up this morning. Like the day I graduated from college and your grandfather told me he was so proud of me. Or the first time your dad made an arrest and he took all of us out for dinner to celebrate."

Aunt Maggie walked over to Gabi and took her hands. "How scared I was that first night you came to live with me because I didn't know how to be the parent you needed."

Tears welled up in Gabi's eyes, and she hugged her aunt. "Aunt Maggie, this is amazing. I'm so happy to see you feeling so good. And you were—are—the best mother I ever could have asked for. I don't know what I would have done without you. After Dad died, I couldn't have lived another day in that house with Monica."

"Your mother did the best—" Aunt Maggie started to say.

"No, she didn't, and you know it," Gabi said. It was an old disagreement. Aunt Maggie had never been willing to condemn Gabi's mother for her behavior, but that hadn't stopped her from taking Gabi in after her father died and the fighting with her mom became a daily occurrence.

"What on earth?"

Gabi turned to see her sister, wide-eyed, outside the kitchen.

"Look, Aunt Maggie's feeling better. Isn't it amazing?"

"Come in, come in," Aunt Maggie said. "Brownies will be ready momentarily. Can I get you some coffee?"

"It's great to see you up and about," Alina said, coming over to give her aunt a one-armed hug. "And yes, I'd love some coffee."

Gabi raised an eyebrow at her sister, who was trying to hide her Starbucks coffee cup behind her back. Alina shrugged, sidled over to the trash can, and dropped the cup in.

A few minutes later, the three women gathered around

the kitchen table, waiting for the brownies to cool enough to dig in. As Aunt Maggie had said, who needs scrambled eggs when you can have freshly baked brownies for breakfast?

"Oh, I forgot to ask," Aunt Maggie said. "What happened with that guy you were going to talk to about your friend?"

Gabi filled her aunt and sister in on her visit with Miguel and the phone call that followed.

"Jesus, Gabriella. You've got to stop taking such stupid risks," Alina said, taking that older sister tone of voice that drove Gabi crazy.

Before she could respond, Aunt Maggie spoke up. "Now, now, I don't think it was stupid. I think your sister is very brave."

"You can be brave and stupid at the same time," Alina said. "And I think butting into a murder investigation definitely qualifies."

"There's probably some truth to that," said Aunt Maggie, placing one hand over Alina's hand and another over Gabi's. "But I don't see anything wrong with asking a few questions. Clearly that meeting was enough to rile someone up. Seems to me, now would be the time to take a step back and let someone else take over."

Gabi looked from her aunt to her sister. Both seemed genuinely concerned. And the last thing she wanted to do was stress her aunt out. Especially now that she seemed to be feeling better.

"I hear you, okay? And I understand why you're both worried. But all I did was ask some questions, and I didn't even get very far. Besides, who knows? Maybe Brendan, if that's even who the caller was, thinks I'm trying to get Miguel as a client and that's why he's trying to scare me off. It might not have anything to do with Connor's murder."

"And if you're wrong?" Alina asked.

Gabi didn't answer right away, and the three quietly nibbled on the still slightly-too-hot brownies. Her mind picked over the bits and pieces of information she knew. What was Connor up to? What did Major know before he was killed? Was Brendan the person who left that voicemail, and what was he threatening her about? She couldn't put it out of her mind.

"I know that look…" Aunt Maggie's voice broke through Gabi's thoughts. "You're not ready to let go of this, are you?"

She shrugged. "I don't know. It's like a buzzing in my brain that won't quiet down. I can't fit any of the pieces together, no matter how I turn them around. There's something missing."

"Sounds like you need a fresh set of eyes," Aunt Maggie said.

"Aunt Maggie! Please, don't encourage her. It's too dangerous."

"Hmm, new eyes." Gabi ignored her sister and idly took another brownie out of the pan. "Who else would know what Connor was up to?"

Alina thumped her hands down on the table in frustration. "I give in. Clearly, you're not ready to let this go." She paused, looking from Aunt Maggie to Gabi. "I can't believe I'm doing this, but…the widow."

"Huh?"

"Connor's widow. Isn't there a chance that she'd have information about his business?"

"Alina, that's genius," Gabi said. "But why would she talk to me? Especially if she believes Major killed her husband. It's no secret that Major and I were friends."

"What if you tell her that you think Major was murdered and that you believe it's the same person that killed Connor," Aunt Maggie suggested.

"That could work. I mean, it can't hurt to try."

"It literally can hurt. These people are dangerous." Alina ran her hand through her hair. "Me and my big mouth. Please, Gabi, just be careful," she said.

"She will," Aunt Maggie said, taking Gabi's hand back in hers. "She knows how much we love her. Now, who needs more coffee?"

As Aunt Maggie went to pour more coffee, Gabi dug around in her purse until she found the napkin that she'd had Miguel write Connor's phone number on. She hoped it was his home number, not some office number that Brendan might answer.

12

"Thank you for the invitation, Deidre," Gabi said.

Already seated after letting them in, their host poured three glasses of iced tea and gestured at the oversized couch. Gabi and Sophia sat. Over their heads, an equally oversize chandelier lit up the room with an unnatural brightness that had Gabi wishing she'd brought sunglasses.

The light didn't help the dull headache that teased the edge of Gabi's consciousness. It had been a late night, after a scare with her aunt—whose burst of energy had lasted less than 48 hours and left Aunt Maggie more spent than before —had left Gabi sitting in a chair watching over her all Monday night. Sophia had insisted on driving as soon as she saw Gabi's face that morning, but she'd spent the entire ride echoing Alina's warning about unnecessary risks. It was a warning Gabi had heard ad nauseum since she had phoned Deidre two days ago.

By the time they'd gotten to the Alexandria suburb where Connor had lived, Gabi was almost ready to throw in the towel—just to get Alina and now Sophia to stop nagging her

—but all her doubts melted away upon pulling up to the garish McMansion.

"Since Connor died, I've barely seen anyone 'cept my brother, so it's nice to have some company."

Gabi examined Deidre's face as she spoke. Though makeup artfully concealed it from afar, up close, Gabi could see that Deidre was older than she'd first assumed.

"We're very sorry for your loss," Gabi said.

"Yes, so… Oh my gosh, I love your shoes," Sophia blurted as she caught sight of Deidre's strappy multi-hued sandals.

Gabi had to remember to close her mouth, she was so surprised at her friend's words. It wasn't the first time a cute pair of shoes had distracted Sophia from a task at hand, though Gabi wasn't sure she could remember a more inappropriate time for Sophia's obsession to hit.

But then Deidre smiled brightly. She was clearly pleased by the compliment, and that could only help them. Before she'd become the designated driver, Sophia had shown up that morning insisting on accompanying Gabi for "protection." Gabi wasn't exactly sure how Sophia intended to protect her if Brendan showed up with murder on his mind. But while she wouldn't admit it to Sophia, she did feel a teeny bit safer having her with her. And it didn't hurt that her friend had a knack for connecting with people.

Deidre waved her hand, dismissing the women's condolences. "T'wasn't much of a loss. I don't think it was too much of a secret that me and Connor were done. He was a right thug and a crook. If he hadn't of died, I'da filed for divorce by now."

Gabi and Sophia exchanged startled glances.

Deidre laughed at the identical expression on their faces. "I've shocked ya, haven't I? To be honest, I hated my husband. And I cannot say I never thought about killing him myself. So actually, I'm grateful to your friend Major, if indeed he did it. I wish I coulda said thank you."

Gabi took a deep breath. Deidre had offered an opening. "Here's the thing, Deidre. I don't believe that Major killed your husband. And I don't believe that Major died of a heart attack either."

"No?" Deidre tensed, her glass of iced tea halfway to her mouth.

"No. I believe someone else killed Connor, and I believe that same someone killed Major as well."

Gabi felt Deidre searching her face, wariness evident in her eyes. "And what is it you're wanting from me?"

"I thought maybe you could tell us more about your husband's business. Like, how did it work? Did he work from home? Did he have any independent contractors? What other suppliers did he sell? That sort of thing."

Deidre laughed again, the wariness replaced by cynicism. "You talk as if Connor actually was a travel agent. He didn't know the first thing about selling travel."

"But he *was* selling SeaCirque," Sophia said, confusion crinkling her eyes.

"Did he sell other cruise lines as well or something other than cruises?" Gabi asked.

"As far as I know, the only company Connor worked with was SeaCirque."

It didn't seem as if Deidre knew very much about Connor's business, but Gabi wasn't ready to give up. Deidre had to know something about how Connor managed to stay in business when he was charging next to nothing for the cruises he sold.

"Deidre, about a year ago, there was an investigation…" Gabi let her words trail off.

"Aye, I know. It was something about stealing clients, no? Can't say I know any more than that. Connor never talked to me about his business. He never talked to me about anything, really. But I can tell you this. Connor never worked an honest day in his life before we moved to Maryland. And I doubt he worked one after we came here."

If Gabi had felt confused after her meeting with Miguel, she was doubly so now. "So what was he doing?" she asked before she could stop herself.

"I don't know. He never told me, and I never asked. Honestly, I never cared, and frankly, I still don't."

Gabi didn't know how to respond to Deidre's bluntness. Or to her lack of concern that her murdered husband's business was starting to seem more and more like a front for something else.

"Why SeaCirque?" Sophia asked, breaking into Gabi's train of thought.

"Now that I do know," Deidre said and paused to sip from her glass. "About four years ago, Connor suddenly up and decided to move us from Brooklyn to here. Said he'd been contacted by someone he knew that worked for this cruise line. They invited him to be an agent and sell a bunch of cruises. Told him he could get rich doing it."

"Do you know who it was?" Gabi cut Deidre off. "What the person's name was?"

"No. He said it was his childhood best friend. I didn't know he'd had any."

"But you said he wasn't actually an agent?" Gabi asked, wondering how anyone thought they could get rich selling cruises. Gabi made a good living, but getting rich? Unlikely.

"I mean, he was doing business. I know there were some group sales or something. Every once in a while, I'd hear him on the phone with some group leader or another talking about room numbers. But I really don't think it was that many. And he certainly wasn't helping anyone with anything. No, Connor was not a travel agent. Not the way you and your friend are."

"What about your brother" Gabi asked.

"What about my brother?" The wary look returned to Deidre's face.

"Well, on the *Sea Fantasy,* your brother told us he was going into business with Connor?"

"Ha! My brother knows even less than Connor did about cruises. Brendan wanted to get in on whatever action Connor had going. But Connor wasn't havin' none of it."

"Yet now that your husband is dead, Brendan seems intent on taking over where Connor left off," Gabi said.

Gabi flinched when Deidre slammed her glass down on the coffee table, and Sophia reached for Gabi's hand.

"So?" Deidre said aggressively this time. "Are you saying you think my brother killed my husband?"

Gabi had realized she was taking a risk the minute the words were out of her mouth, but she hadn't been prepared for the fury in Deidre's voice. "No, no. I'm not saying that. It's, well, your brother threatened Major in the days leading up to his death. He told him to stay away from Connor's business if he wanted to stay healthy. And then, well, Major suddenly dies, and then three days ago, I get an almost identical phone call."

Gabi held Deidre's angry stare for as long as she could.

"I'm the last person on earth who would tell you my brother is a saint. But you know what? Why don't you ask him yerself?" She leaned back slightly and yelled over her shoulder, "Brendan!"

Gabi and Sophia held their collective breaths, hoping Deidre was bluffing.

"Aye, what do you want?" Brendan's deep voice echoed from around a corner.

"There are some ladies here who'd like to ask you a few questions."

Sophia's hand spasmed at the sound of his voice, her pink-polished nails digging into Gabi's skin.

"No, that's okay. Really," Gabi tried to say. "I'm sure you're both busy. We should probably be getting on the road."

"Oh, but you just got here, and you drove all this way. It would be a shame if you didn't get to ask *all* your questions."

Sophia whimpered as Brendan rounded the corner. The last time Gabi had seen him, at the hotel in Baltimore, had been from across the room. Up close, he towered over where they sat on the couch. He had a beer in one hand, and with the other, he was rhythmically squeezing a hand gripper.

"Who the hell are you?" Brendan asked.

"I… I'm Gabi Feraru. We met briefly on the *Sea Fantasy*," Gabi said.

"Well, I don't remember ya. What do you want with me?"

Well, that's odd, Gabi thought in a moment of rationality amidst the fear playing staccato with her pulse. She was almost positive that he was the one who'd left her the threatening voicemail. He should know exactly who she was. With Sophia still gripping her wrist, Gabi stood, pulling her friend up with her. Brendan towered over them, but it would be easier to move away from him if they were standing.

"We were just asking Deidre some questions about Connor's business, trying to understand what he was up to. You mentioned on the cruise that you and Connor were going into business together. With him dead, well, we…I… thought you might know something."

Brendan stepped closer, and it took all of Gabi's

willpower not to backstep. Briefly, she wondered if he could see the skin beneath her right eye start to flicker in time with her pulse. It was an involuntary tic that stress had always triggered in her. Thankfully, her annoyance at the tic brought her back from the edge of panic. She forced herself to breathe, shifting her weight forward so she'd be able to spring back easily if needed.

"Not that it's any of your business, but Connor died before we could, ah, finalize our business arrangement."

"Right, but now that he's dead, didn't that drop his business into your lap? I mean, that worked out pretty well for you." The words were out of Gabi's mouth before she realized she'd spoken.

Brendan didn't answer right away. He stared at her then slowly took another, large step forward. This time, Gabi did backstep, pushing Sophia behind her as she did.

"If you mean that my sister didn't have to go through all the hassle of a divorce and still got to walk away with everything? Then, aye, it worked out great for us."

"And his business…" Gabi prompted.

"I think that's enough questions," he said, stepping forward yet again, forcing Gabi and Sophia to step around the sofa to keep their distance.

"What about your threats to Major?" Gabi asked. She was surprised her voice had been able to make noise, considering how tight her throat felt.

"And to Gabi," Sophia's voice came out as a near squeak.

Brendan smiled. "What about them?"

Deidre finally stood as well, her face red. "You said the call to you was three days ago?" she asked. "Then it wasn't my brother. He was in custody with immigration. Seems someone gave them an anonymous tip that he was wanted by the UK government for some bombings dating back to The

Troubles. Only, whoever it was, was lying. Our lawyer only got him out yesterday."

"Now, I think it *is* time you left," Brendan practically growled, and before Gabi could react, he was standing over them. He'd dropped the hand gripper on the sofa and had Gabi's shoulder enclosed firmly, and painfully, in his beefy fist as he pushed her backwards.

"Okay, okay. No need for—" Gabi tried to say, but they were outside with the door slammed shut behind them before she could finish her sentence. Gabi rubbed her shoulder.

"That probably could have gone better," she said.

"How's your aunt doing?"

Gabi looked from Sophia to the ceiling, picturing Aunt Maggie sleeping in the bedroom above them. She'd done little more than sleep since her surge of energy three days ago. Gabi hadn't even been able to get her to the hospital for treatments. The doctors wanted her to be moved to the hospital, but Gabi knew that wasn't what her aunt wanted.

She lowered her voice, even though she knew their voices wouldn't carry upstairs. "Not so well. The radiation is taking more and more out of her, and the doctors say the treatments don't seem to be working. Her last MRI showed no sign of shrinkage. She wants to stop the radiation."

Sophia, who was sitting next to Gabi at the table, slipped her hand over Gabi's and squeezed.

"I'm so sorry to hear that." Jill's voice came out of the phone, set to speaker, sitting on the dining table.

"It sucks, for sure, but I still believe there's hope. She's supposed to start another round of chemo in a couple of days. Maybe the chemo will be better than the radiation." Gabi coughed to cover the catch in her throat.

"But how are you? Shouldn't you be popping any day now?" Sophia asked while Gabi blinked back tears.

"I sure hope so. Every day I think today has got to be the day. I don't think my stomach can stretch any farther!"

Back in control of herself, Gabi recounted their visit with Deidre to Jill. Though she knew someone at the cruise line wasn't trustworthy, she didn't believe it was Jill and had decided to ask for her help. "If Connor wasn't a travel advisor like his wife said, and he wasn't selling a huge number of cruises, then how was he making money? What was he up to?"

Gabi and Sophia had already discussed their reactions to the meeting with Deidre and Brendan on the drive back from Virginia. They had a theory.

Jill spoke slowly, seeming to iron out her thoughts as she did. "So according to Connor's wife, someone at SeaCirque asked Connor to come down to Virginia and work as a travel advisor."

"You mean *pose* as a travel advisor," Sophia interrupted.

"That seems to be the implication. And yet, according to SeaCirque's records, Connor Foley was a top seller."

"But according to his wife, he barely sold any cruises," Gabi pointed out.

Jill picked up the thought. "Meaning someone, presumably the person who invited him to work with SeaCirque, was somehow making it look like he was selling more than he was."

Gabi and Sophia looked at each other then back at the phone. Gabi fiddled with a pen by popping the cap off and then pushing it back on. Sophia chewed on her bottom lip.

"But why? That's the question." Jill paused again. "At the very least, it's fraud."

"One hundred percent," Gabi said. "But Sophia and I think there might be more to it."

"Well, if I've learned anything from watching too much crime TV, fraud combined with a fake company usually means one thing. Money laundering."

Gabi's fingers stilled on the pen she was holding.

"Or embezzlement."

13

―――――

"The cruise line is telling us they can't put us in a suite, even though that's what I booked. I want this fixed immediately."

Gabi tried to concentrate on the woman on the phone. Only ten minutes ago, she and Sophia had been searching through the SeaCirque website, trying to find biographical information on the line's sales reps to see if any were originally from New York City like Connor. Now she was listening to an irate stranger who was demanding she fix a mistake one of the many online travel agencies had made.

"Ma'am, I'm sorry I can't help you. Since we did not make the reservation for you, we can't make any changes to it, nor can we call the company on your behalf. Next time, I would suggest you contact a travel advisor first, instead of booking online."

"But what do I do about my reservation? I leave in two days, and I refuse to stay in a mini-suite."

"Did you try calling the customer service number for the online agency you booked with?"

"Hrmph." The woman hung up.

"That's what you get when you try to save a few bucks," Gabi muttered. "Come on, Soph. Let's keep looking."

It had been two days since their visit with Deidre, and neither had quite given up their belief that Brendan was involved in the murders, despite what Connor's wife had told them. And since they'd seen Brendan and John in a hushed conversation the day Connor died, Sophia was now convinced John was the mysterious partner.

"But why don't you think it's John?" Sophia asked.

"Because he's from Ireland, that's why. Deidre said the person who called Connor was an old childhood friend. So, it can't be John. It has to be someone who grew up in Brooklyn."

"She could have been lying. Do me a favor and look him up anyway," Sophia said.

"Fine, but don't get pissed at me when I say I told you so." Gabi pulled up John's bio.

Looking over Gabi's shoulder, Sophia read aloud. "Born in Shannon, Ireland, John Clarke moved to Brooklyn, New York when he was eight years old. He has been with SeaCirque for 15 years and is based in Washington, D.C."

"Ha!" Sophia said.

"So that whole accent thing is a put on?" Gabi shook her head in amazement.

"See, *I* told you. Wait, who are you looking up now?"

"I'm curious about something."

"A graduate of the elite private school system in Rhode Island, Stefan Davidson attended the Ross School of Business at the University of Michigan. He is based in SeaCirque's Miami headquarters," Gabi read aloud.

"Stefan? Just because you don't particularly like the guy for not helping Major doesn't make him a murderer or an embezzler. I'm telling you, it's John Clarke."

"It's definitely possible." Gabi clicked the back button,

returning to John's online bio. "What about that woman?" she asked.

"What woman? Deidre?"

"No, the one on the ship that told Connor he owed her money. Do you think she worked for SeaCirque?"

"Wearing short shorts? I doubt it. I really think it's John."

"But how can we know for sure?" Gabi asked, still not entirely convinced.

"Maybe *we* don't," Sophia said. "This seems like the perfect time to call the FBI with what we've learned."

Here we go again. Gabi sighed. "Not yet. Everything we have is circumstantial. We don't have any proof of anything, including that John and Connor even knew each other before SeaCirque."

"Circumstantial? What is this, *Law & Order*?"

"Dad. Cop."

"Fine, then what do you suggest?"

Gabi tugged on a strand of hair that she'd pulled out of her ponytail. "Do you remember, a couple of weeks ago, we got an e-mail about upcoming changes to SeaCirque's online booking system?"

"Vaguely."

"What if I asked John to come here and give us a live demo of the changes? Then while he's here, I bring Connor up and see if they knew each other?"

"Just like that? Come straight out and ask, 'Hey did you know Connor as a boy, and if so, were you guys embezzling from SeaCirque together? Oh, and did you kill him too?'"

"Sarcasm doesn't become you, Soph. No, I'll find a subtle way to work it into conversation and go from there."

"I don't know, Gabi. It seems dangerous. If he is the guy who killed Connor and Major, what's to stop him from killing you too?"

"You."

"Me?" Sophia's question was practically a squeak.

"This isn't going to work," Sophia said for the fourth time the next morning. "He's going to know I'm here, and he's not going to say anything." Despite her misgivings, Sophia had dressed for the occasion, as she always did. Clad head to toe in black, she looked ready for some cat burglary. The only problem was that Bugsy, who had been sitting on her lap since they got in that morning, had shed quite a bit of gray fur on her jumpsuit. Gabi was more simply dressed in black jeans and a *follow the white rabbit* T-shirt, and, since Bugsy still didn't trust her, she wasn't cloaked in gray fur.

"No, he's not going to notice anything. The light'll be off, and he'll be facing away from you. He'll have no idea there's anyone else in the office."

"And what if he pulls out a gun? What am I supposed to do?"

"He's not going to pull out a gun. He isn't stupid." Gabi forestalled Sophia's next question. "And if he does try something, you immediately call 911, walk out of the bathroom, and announce that the police are on their way."

Sophia stood up from her chair, dumping Bugsy onto the floor. "I'm scared."

"I am too, but think about it this way. We're not confronting John about killing anyone. I still think Brendan makes more sense as the actual killer. We're simply trying to find out if he knew Connor. If we can confirm that, then we can go to the FBI, okay?"

Sophia sighed. "I guess so."

"John's supposed to be here in ten minutes. Take your bag with you into the bathroom. Leave the door cracked."

With Sophia hidden in the restroom and Bugsy curled

up under Sophia's desk, Gabi tried to settle down at her desk. She wanted to look busy with work and unconcerned with anything else when John arrived. But no matter how hard she tried to concentrate, she couldn't focus on the files in front of her. Or calm the butterflies in her stomach. It was a relief when John finally walked through the door.

"Wow, right on time," Gabi said, possibly too energetically. "Did you have any trouble getting here or finding parking?"

"Not at all. And how are you this fine mornin'?"

Liar! Gabi wanted to call John out on his fake accent right there and then. Instead, she forced herself to smile. The last thing she needed was to make John suspicious of her motives for asking him to stop by. "I'm okay. Thanks for driving all this way and on such short notice. I want to get a handle on the changes to the reservation system as quickly as I can, and in-person is so much better than via Zoom."

"Of course. That's what I'm here for. Luckily, the changes really aren't that drastic." Over the next twenty minutes, John walked Gabi through the new res system. In spite of her real reason for having John come to the office, Gabi found the demo useful and noted a few items to show to Sophia – and Lewis if he ever showed up any time soon – later on.

"That wasn't too bad, was it?"

"No, actually, it wasn't. You're a good teacher."

"Ah, don't be making me blush now."

"I love your accent. It's amazing you still have one since you came to the States so young."

John raised an eyebrow, and Gabi shrugged. "When Jill told me you were going to be her replacement, I looked you up."

"I keep askin'…asking them to take that bit down. I think the accent helps me connect with my clients better. Especially the ladies," John added, winking.

Gabi faked a laugh. "Yeah, I guess a Brooklyn accent isn't as sexy."

Meooow.

"You have a cat?" John craned his neck around to look. Gabi realized Bugsy was in the bathroom, most likely trying to get Sophia's attention.

"Um, yes. Bugsy. Bugsy? Come here, Bugsy." Gabi clucked her tongue. "He's probably hungry." Gabi jumped out of her chair and grabbed the bag of Iams Sophia kept on the bottom shelf of the bookcase by her desk. Shaking the bag loudly first, Gabi poured a handful of morsels into a small bowl. As she'd hoped, the sound of food distracted Bugsy from Sophia's presence, and he trotted out of the bathroom.

"See, hungry." Gabi felt more out of breath than she should have. She hoped John didn't notice. "So, where were we? Right, Brooklyn." She ignored the perplexed look on John's face. "Wasn't that advisor that died on the *Sea Fantasy* from Brooklyn? What was his name? Conrad?"

"Connor." Gabi noticed John's nostrils flare as he said Connor's name.

"Did you know him?"

"I think all of SeaCirque's reps knew of Connor. He had quite a reputation. You were there for his…er…performance at the naming, weren't you?"

"Yeah." Gabi brushed off John's question. "But did you know him? From Brooklyn, I mean."

"Brooklyn's a big borough, Gabi," John said and started packing up his laptop.

It was now or never, Gabi thought. "I only ask because I saw you talking to Connor's brother-in-law on the ship. When I was doing the ship tour. I waved at you, remember?"

John finished packing, practically shoving his notebook into his backpack. Then he paused, looking down at his bag, though Gabi didn't think he was actually seeing it. "I believe it was your pretty friend that waved. But, aye, I knew Connor from Brooklyn. Him and my sister used to date. And he wasn't very nice to her, if you get my meaning. Brendan found me on the ship and told me that Connor's wife was filing for divorce. She'd told him about Mary—my sister—and he wanted to know if, maybe, she'd be willing to give them an affidavit about Connor's temper."

"That's… God, I'm sorry."

"It all happened a long time ago. And I guess what goes around comes around."

That's a bit harsh, Gabi thought, as she watched John pull himself back into the present.

"Now, I better be goin'. I've got two more appointments in this area and then a long drive back to D.C."

That wasn't enough information, Gabi thought. This might be her only chance to find out if John was the one who'd invited Connor to sell SeaCirque.

"Right, right. Had you spoken to Connor over the years?" she asked.

"No, we weren't friends before he dated my sister, and we certainly weren't after."

"Oh, then how did your sister and Connor meet?"

John buckled up the straps of his backpack. "She was friends with Connor's sister, Megan."

"Connor had a sister? Where is she now?"

"Megan? Haven't talked to her in ages. Pretty sure she's still in New York. Last I heard, she worked at the New York City library. Listen, call me if you have any questions about the new res system. And here's an invitation to a special dinner SeaCirque will be hosting in New York City next Saturday. Sorry for the late notice, but they just told us about it."

He handed a glossy postcard-sized invite to Gabi,

grabbed his bag, and walked in the direction of the bathroom.

"Wait, what are you—"

Gabi reacted too slowly, and John flicked on the switch in the bathroom, revealing Sophia dressed all in black and sitting on the toilet, lid down, with a ballpoint hammer in her hand.

Sophia startled, jumped up, and drew back her arm as if to brandish the hammer. But in her haste, she fumbled and the hammer fell forward, dropping onto John's foot.

"Ow! Are you serious?" he yelled, stepping backwards out of the bathroom.

"I'm so sorry. Are you okay? Sophia was just…was just…" Gabi looked to Sophia, who had frozen with her arm halfway back when the hammer fell.

If Sophia's body was frozen in place, her eyes were not. They darted back and forth between Gabi and John. "We have a leak and I was going to fix it," Sophia finally said. "But then you got here and I didn't want to make a lot of noise." Her words trailed off, and she looked at John, her eyes wide and face splotchy red from embarrassment.

John looked from Sophia to Gabi to the hammer and then back to the women. Slowly, without taking his eyes off them, he bent down to pick up the hammer.

"Were you spying on me?" he asked, his face red. He held the hammer firmly as if he might swing it at them at any moment.

"No, of course not." Sophia's squeak was back.

"I wouldn't call it spying," Gabi replied at the same time. She held her hands in front of her, partly in a plea for forgiveness and partly to ward off a swing from the hammer.

Again, John looked from the women to the hammer he now held. He walked over to Gabi's desk and placed it on top of it.

"You think I had something to do with Connor's death." It wasn't a question, and he didn't wait for a reply. "All those questions about did I know Connor? You think I killed him."

Gabi tried to interrupt, but John talked loudly over her denial. "Screw you. You're both crazy. Everyone knows it was your friend Major who killed Connor. Go on, try to deny it. Tell me all those questions weren't because you think I killed Connor."

Gabi tried to think of something, anything to say, but her mind stayed blank, and so she kept silent.

"That's what I thought." He shook his head and walked towards the exit. Just before leaving, he turned back to Gabi and Sophia. "You know what? Maybe you should find yourselves another BDM."

Gabi and Sophia stood, still frozen in place, as he stormed out the door.

"Oh wow, does he hate you," Sophia finally said.

"Probably. But who cares? He just told us he has a powerful motive for wanting Connor dead!"

14

WITHOUT THE AIR CONDITIONER ON, the temperature in the room hovered above 90. Gabi sat cross legged on a chair by her aunt's bed, wearing a pair of purple boxer shorts and a unicorn-emblazoned spaghetti strap tank top. It was too hot for anything else. A box of tissues sat on the floor, and every so often, she leaned down to grab one and wipe her brow. Glancing out of the window, she briefly gave thanks that it was a gray, overcast day. Without cloud cover, the afternoon sun would have been streaming into the room, baking it even further. She plucked an invoice from the pile of papers on her lap and fanned herself with it. She hoped the rain that had been threatening since that morning would finally come.

"Why not take a break in a room with AC?"

Gabi startled at the voice behind her, and at the same time, her aunt mumbled, "No air conditioner, please. It's too cold."

Alina stepped into the room, and Gabi scooted over to her aunt's side.

"No, no, Aunt Maggie, the air conditioner is off. Are you cold? Should I get you another blanket?" Aunt Maggie was already buried under a down comforter and a throw. "Aunt Maggie?"

Gabi's aunt opened her eyes briefly and focused on Gabi's face. She smiled, and then her eyes closed and she slipped back into the restless sleep state that had become her norm. Next to her, Gabi heard Alina's sharp inhale, and she looked up. Alina had stopped inside the doorway, staring at Aunt Maggie. Gabi could see the tears gathering at the corners of her eyes.

"I didn't realize… I mean, she was just making brownies a few days ago."

Gabi paused. As close as she and her sister had gotten over the past year and a half, she still didn't quite trust her not to tell their mom what was going on—especially knowing their mother would try to browbeat Gabi into letting her take over Aunt Maggie's care.

"It started two days after that, this sleeping thing. She barely wakes up anymore. Her doctor wants her to be moved into the hospital."

Alina sniffed and rubbed an eye with the back of her hand. "You should have told me. Why haven't you moved her yet?"

Gabi's muscles tensed. "She's scheduled for a chemotherapy treatment on Monday. I decided it could wait until then. I'm paying the visiting nurse to come in for a few hours today and tomorrow to help me."

"That's four days from now," Alina said. "I don't think we should wait that long."

"We?" Gabi snapped, decades' worth of anger erupting from inside her, despite their newfound closeness. "Since when is there a 'we' when it comes to Aunt Maggie? Until two years ago, when was the last time you even spoke to her? No, Aunt Maggie raised me when Monica kicked me out. I will make whatever decisions need to be made."

The argument was an old one, but time hadn't dulled any of the emotions involved.

"For Pete's sake, would you stop with that? Mom didn't kick you out. And she's my aunt too. I've loved getting to know her again. So, if the doctor said she needs to go to the hospital, then I think she needs to go."

"She will. On Monday," Gabi said.

"Gabriella," Alina started to say.

"Alina," Gabi said before she could finish. The sisters faced off for a few seconds before Alina turned her gaze back to Aunt Maggie, conceding defeat.

"Will she… I mean, do you think she'll ever come home again?"

Gabi's vision blurred, and she blinked her eyes a few times then cleared her throat and straightened the blankets around her aunt. "It really is hot in here. Why don't we go downstairs?"

Gabi grabbed two bottles of diet peach Snapple from the fridge, and they settled onto the couch in the living room.

"Gabi," Alina began hesitantly. It was clear to Gabi that her sister didn't want to start another fight, but she had that *I know better than you* look that she copied so perfectly from their mom. "I know I'm not as close to Aunt Maggie as you are and that it's only because of you that I even have a relationship with her now. But I can help. You don't have to do this alone."

Gabi stared out a window, watching a squirrel dig through the lawn, looking for acorns, but it was still summer, and none were to be found.

"I know you mean well, Alina. And I really do appreciate it. But it's been only Aunt Maggie and me for so long. Honestly, it was a little hard watching you guys become close. I don't think I can… Aunt Maggie took care of me when I needed it. Now it's my turn to take care of her. I hope you can understand."

"I do. Just remember, I'm here if you need me."

Gabi nodded, and the two fell into silence.

"Sophia tells me you think John Clarke is the guy that travel advisor was working with," Alina said.

"When did you see Sophia?" Gabi asked, annoyed that her best friend had blabbed to Alina.

"At the bagel shop this morning. So, do you?"

"It makes sense. I mean, he works for the cruise line, so he's probably got all kinds of access to the reservation system. Maybe he can fix prices or force commission payments or something else like that, in order to make it all look normal. Plus, his history with Connor goes way back. And, if we believe what he said, he had a real reason to hate Connor."

"Sophia said he didn't look like a killer."

"Since when do killers look like killers? No one had any clue about Ted Bundy. And besides, she was the one who thought it was him in the first place."

"Don't you think it's finally time for you to call the FBI about this?" Alina asked.

"I don't know. It still doesn't feel like enough. If I call the FBI and they think I'm a crackpot, I could do more harm than good."

"You know what I think?" Alina didn't wait for Gabi to respond. "I think getting involved in all this"—she waved her hands in the air—"is your way of avoiding what's going on up there." She pointed at the ceiling, indicating the bedroom above them.

"I'm sorry. Since when did you become a psychiatrist?"

Alina smiled and crossed her arms. "You know what? That's not a bad idea. I should finish my psychology degree I started all those years ago, and then you, Sophia, and I can team up. Come in to have your head shrunk and book a vacation to Aruba while you're at it. What do you think?"

"I think we were talking about John Clarke," Gabi said.

"No, we were talking about you avoiding Aunt Maggie's death."

"Aunt Maggie might still recover. And I'm getting involved because Violet asked me to and because Major was my friend."

Alina shook her head. "So why not go to the FBI with what you know? *That* would help Violet."

"Because I don't have any proof of anything. And I'm not willing to risk making things worse for Major if there's any chance the FBI will think I'm crazy."

"Worse for Major? How? He's dead!"

Gabi suppressed an urge to hit her sister. "You know what I mean."

"So, what do you propose?" Alina asked.

"John mentioned Connor has a sister in the Bronx. What if I talked to her and she could confirm what John and Deidre told us?"

"What do you mean?"

"I mean, what if she can tell me Connor and John were best friends *and* that Connor did date John's sister and was abusive to her? Then, at least, we'd also know John wasn't lying. And most importantly, we'd have actual proof of a motive that I could take to the FBI."

"And what if she doesn't remember John or his sister?"

"Then we're back to where we started."

Gabi felt more excited than she'd ever felt before. She'd figured out who did it, in what room, and with what weapon, and she

couldn't wait to tell her dad. He'd be so proud of her. "His little detective," he always called her.

Too impatient to wait for the elevator, she raced up three flights of stairs to the cancer ward. The normally heavy door felt light as she flung it open and ran down the hall.

"Daddy," she yelled. "Daddy, I figured it out."

Her momentum halted abruptly as she collided with a man carrying bed sheets. Her nose wrinkled as she pushed past him. The sheets smelled funny.

"Daddy, I figured it out," dream Gabi repeated, but then she pulled up short. Daddy wasn't there. The Clue box that was always on his lap, ready for when she came from school, was sitting on the chair in the corner.

Gabi struggled to wake up as dream Gabi's confusion muddled her thoughts. Her sheets were sweat-soaked, despite the A/C, and had tangled around her legs. Instinctively, as she had done every morning since she was thirteen and had moved in with Aunt Maggie to escape her mother, she listened for the sound of Light FM drifting up from downstairs and inhaled for the sweet smell of vanilla coffee. Dead silence and the acrid smell of her own sweat was all she got. Afraid to make a noise, as if doing so would break some magical spell holding everything in place, Gabi muffled her sobs with her pillow.

Two hours later, under gray clouds still threatening but not delivering rain, Gabi pulled out of her driveway. Images of her dad's last days and memories of their Clue games floated through her thoughts. She'd never played Clue again. In fact, she hadn't even enjoyed puzzles of any kind ever since. A therapist Aunt Maggie had insisted she go to had told her that puzzles reminded her of her dad's death. Her response to that had simply been, "Whatever."

"And yet, here I am trying to unravel a real-life puzzle,"

she muttered to herself as she approached the stoplight by the train station, where she usually parked her car. When she put her foot on the brake, the car didn't slow down.

Though she wasn't going fast, only about thirty miles an hour, there was a car ahead of her. She pressed on the brakes again. Nothing. Cold numbness spread down to her finger-tips as she realized she was seconds away from plowing into the car in front of her.

Without thinking, she swerved to the right, straight into a no-parking sign. Fortunately, no one was on the sidewalk, and though the sign bent due to the force of her car, it didn't break. Passers-by heard the loud crash of the impact, but all Gabi heard was the loud whoosh of the air bag deploying, smacking her in the face and bringing instant tears to her eyes.

What felt like hours later but was most likely no more than a few seconds, Gabi became aware of someone knocking on the driver's-side window of her car.

"Are you okay?" a man asked. She couldn't hear him through the ringing in her ears, but she recognized the o and k his lips formed.

Gabi brought her hand to her face, which was wet with tears and, when she looked down at her hands, blood. At the sight of the blood, she suddenly felt the sting in her nose and wondered if it was broken.

Slowly, she pushed the now deflated airbag to the side and fumbled for the door handle. Still, her ears were ringing. Even as she opened the door, the words the man who'd been knocking on her window spoke to her sounded muffled. She tried to step outside to get away from the car, but she couldn't get out of her seat. Panic blossomed, and her eyes darted to her legs. She expected to see them crushed by the dashboard.

"You have your seat belt on," the man yelled, stretching across her body to click the button and set her free.

She tumbled out of the car in her haste to escape. Asphalt dug into her palms, bringing fresh tears. Her breath came fast, and when she tried to stand, she swayed, spurring the man who'd undone her seat belt to grab her. He walked her over to the curb and sat her down.

Gabi's thoughts spun. Her eyes darted from her car, the front of which sported a huge dent from hitting the parking sign, to her bloodied hands.

"Miss, are you okay? Can you hear me?" the man asked.

She struggled to focus. She could hear him now, but the words made no sense.

Flashing lights slowly cut through her confusion. A police car had pulled up in front of her. *I've been in an accident.* It was the first coherent thought she was able to hold on to.

A police officer knelt by her side. "Gabi, are you okay?"

It was Sergeant Don Lindser, an on-again, off-again client who called her every five years to plan a milestone anniversary vacation for his wife. Once upon a time, they'd been surprises, but by the time he planned their fifteenth wedding anniversary trip, his wife had caught on.

"Two more years until your twenty-fifth," she said.

"Gabi, look at me. I need you to concentrate."

She looked at him. Squinted. Focused on his eyes, his lips. "I think I was in an accident," she finally said.

"Yes, you hit the no-parking sign. Do you know what happened?"

Gabi tried to think. She remembered the feel of the brake touching the floor of the car. Nausea welled up in her throat. "The brakes. The brakes didn't work. I was going to hit the car in front of me," she said, wrapping her arms around her stomach, tears flowing more steadily now down her cheeks.

"You're okay, Gabi. You did the right thing. Your car's a little messed up, but..."

"It could have been so much worse," she finished his thought for him.

15

————

Sophia was with a client when Gabi entered the agency later that day. Sergeant Lindser had taken her statement, and AAA had come to take her car to a garage.

Thankful she didn't have to face Sophia yet, and not ready to think about her close call, Gabi dove into the workload that was waiting for her on her desk. She knew she'd eventually have to own up to Sophia—and herself. Without a car, she had no way to get home at day's end, and there was no hiding that. And the way her right eye was still throbbing, she was pretty sure she'd be sporting a black eye by the end of the day. She was going to need Sophia's help to cover that up. Alina would freak out if she saw Gabi with a black eye.

Gabi grabbed the morning mail from Elaine's desk and began sorting through it. Most of it was brochures from travel suppliers trying to catch their attention, but buried in between the glossy pamphlets, flyers, and booklets was a commission check they'd been waiting for. There was also a note card from Miguel Rodriguez, thanking her for meeting with him and wishing her well. Gabi had to run to the bathroom to stop Sophia's client from seeing her tear up.

"Get ahold of yourself girl," she scolded her image in the mirror. "This isn't helping anyone." She splashed a little cold water on her face, ignored the red blotches on her cheek that the air bag had left behind, and went back to where she'd dropped her bag. Digging through it, she found the scrap of paper on which she'd written Connor's sister's name.

As she stared at the paper, a thought flashed through her mind. It was the same thought that had been teasing its way through her brain since the accident. Someone didn't want her digging into Connor's death, or Major's. First there had been the phone call. And now, had the accident been another warning? Or worse? What if her brakes had failed on the highway instead of a local street?

Bile rose up in her throat. Tears leaked from her eyes. She'd always been the kind of person who cried when she got angry during a confrontation. It was a character trait she hated about herself, but this time, she let the anger bubble up and let the heat fill up her cheeks. She wiped away her tears but not the anger.

"Someone doesn't want me to find you, Megan Foley," she said to herself. "Well, screw them. No one kills a friend of mine and walks away." She pulled up Google to find the New York Public Library's website then crawled the site, looking for a page that listed the librarians. Nothing. Next, she tried Googling Megan Foley but got a million results.

"What would Daddy have done?" she asked herself. *Well, he probably wouldn't have been using the Internet, since he died well before most people were using it regularly,* her sarcastic inner voice replied.

Gabi clicked back to the New York Public Library's home page, picked up the phone, and dialed the library's main number.

"New York Public Library. How may I direct your call?"

"Hello. My name is Gabi Feraru. I'm a…a lawyer for a

Mr. Connor Foley, who recently died. I'm trying to locate his sister, Megan Foley, who is a librarian with you. Would you be able to tell me which library she works at?"

"Can you hold a minute?"

"Of course." Gabi drummed her fingers on the desk until she noticed Sophia glaring at her. *Sorry,* she mouthed.

"Mrs. Feraru, thank you for holding. We don't have a Megan Foley, but there is a Megan Riley working as a branch librarian at the Woodlawn Heights library. The number there is…"

Gabi hurriedly copied down the number and thanked the woman on the other end of the phone. Could Megan Riley be Megan Foley? Gabi went back to Google. It took less than fifteen minutes to find a reference to a marriage between Megan Foley and Douglas Riley.

Now sure that she had the right person, she picked up the phone then put it down again. Would it be better to call first or show up unannounced? Which would most likely get her the answers she wanted?

Saturday morning at 10:00, Gabi pulled open the heavy metal door of the Woodlawn Heights library. The whole building was painted green, perhaps in homage to the Irish people who made up the bulk of the local community.

Gabi was surprised at how crowded the library was. Who used libraries anymore? Yet all the computer stations were occupied, and people were scattered throughout the stacks of books or flipping through the morning papers. A young woman was checking out books at the circulation desk near the entrance. Farther inside, Gabi could see a youngish man, probably of Irish descent if his red hair was any indication, seated at an information desk. Gabi had called the library back to find out whether Megan Riley would be working today and had been told she was. She knew Megan was somewhere in the library.

She pushed through the turnstile entrance and got behind two people waiting to speak to the young man. She couldn't help but smile when the woman in front of her began arguing with the librarian over a buck twenty late book fee.

I guess travel clients aren't the only people to quibble over a few dollars, she thought.

After two minutes of back and forth, the man finally agreed to waive half the fee, obviously more in an attempt to get rid of the woman than because he thought she was right. He sighed as Gabi stepped forward.

"How can I help you?"

"I'm looking for Mrs. Riley?"

"She's in the back room. Give me a sec, and I'll call her." He didn't bother to ask Gabi her name or what she wanted.

Gabi stepped aside to allow a teenage girl behind her to approach the desk. She listened in as the girl asked for the CliffsNotes version of *Othello*.

Not long after, a heavyset woman with auburn hair, pale skin liberally sprinkled with freckles, and gunmetal gray–rimmed glasses exited a door near the circulation desk. Gabi immediately saw the family resemblance. The woman's scowl was almost identical to Connor's.

The young man at the info desk caught her eye and pointed with his chin at Gabi.

"Is there a problem?" Megan Riley asked.

"Um, no." Gabi pushed a strand of hair behind her ear and dropped her gaze for a moment. "My name is Gabi Feraru, and I'd like to speak with you about your brother, Connor."

The woman's start was miniscule. If Gabi hadn't been

looking at her closely, afraid of how she might react, she would have missed it. A micro-second later, a tightening around her eyes was all that remained of her reaction.

"He's dead," Megan said without inflection.

Gabi wasn't sure how to respond. "Riiight, that's sort of why I wanted to speak to you." Her eyes did a quick circle of the room. "Is there somewhere a bit quieter we could speak?"

"I haven't spoken to Connor in years."

"I'm sorry, Mrs. Riley."

"Ms. Riley."

"Ms. Riley. It's really important I speak with you. Please."

The branch librarian stared at Gabi for a moment before turning on her heel and heading back the way she had come. "Follow me," she said over her shoulder.

Gabi followed Megan to a desk in the rear of the small office.

"Grab a chair."

Once she was settled into a torn leather desk chair, Gabi didn't know where to begin.

"So?" Megan sat with her elbows on the desk, hands clasped below her chin.

"Ms. Riley, I was a friend of the man who's been accused of murdering your brother." Gabi paused, expecting a reaction from the woman across from her. She didn't get one.

"I'm not sure if you know, but my friend died a month ago."

Megan's eyes flicked to a spot behind Gabi's head, and Gabi felt like she was losing her attention.

"Though the police think he had a heart attack, I don't believe that. I believe that whoever killed your brother also killed my friend."

Megan raised an eyebrow. She pushed three pens together on her desk and aligned the bottoms. "Go on," she said without looking up.

"I've been… Well, I've sort of been looking into Connor's past. Trying to figure out why someone would want to kill him."

"Lots of people had lots of reasons to want Connor dead," Megan said.

"That may be true, but I'm convinced his death had something to do with his, um, career as a travel advisor."

Megan's arm jerked. "Hah, my brother was no more a travel agent than I'm the queen of England. He never put in an honest day of work in his whole life."

"And yet somehow, he ended up in Virginia, selling cruises on SeaCirque Cruise Line. Do you have any idea how that happened?"

"Like I said, Ms. Feraru—"

"Gabi, please."

Megan folded her arms across her chest, glanced at the clock on the wall next to Gabi, and huffed loudly. "Like I said, I hadn't spoken to Connor in years, even before he picked up and left New York. I really don't see how I can be of any help."

"Here's the thing. I spoke with Connor's wife, and she told me that an old friend of Connor's from childhood was responsible for getting him involved in whatever he was doing."

"Did she tell you his name?"

"No, she didn't know it. I thought maybe you could help, you know, tell me more about some of his childhood friends. Then I could see if any of them work at SeaCirque."

Megan unfolded her arms. "If this person you're trying to find really did kill my brother and your friend, aren't you treading in dangerous territory by snooping around?"

"Major was my friend." Gabi glanced at her hands clasped together in her lap. Her right eye still throbbed from yesterday's car accident, but concealer made it easier for her to forget the dangers everyone kept reminding her about. She took a quick breath then another, deeper one and lifted her head to face Megan. "The FBI have all but closed the book on his guilt. That's not right. If my snooping around can somehow change that, then it's something I have to do."

Megan removed her glasses and placed them on the desk. She pulled her chair closer, letting her elbows rest on the desk. "A friend from childhood, you say? He had a lot of friends when we were growing up. Did Deidre give you any information about him at all?"

There was warmth in Megan's voice when she said her sister-in-law's name.

"Not really. She only said Connor had told her the guy had been his best friend when they were kids."

"His best friend? Hmm, I wonder." Megan fell silent a moment, thinking. Gabi watched her mouth slowly curl upwards and her face soften with memories.

"Connor's best friend from the time he was little until he was eleven was a kid named Liam Mulrooney. Liam had come over from Ireland with his mother when he was pretty young. Nice enough boy, older than Connor by a couple of years and a bit conceited."

"Conceited?" That didn't mesh with what Gabi knew of John. Of course, neither did the name Liam.

"Yep." Megan nodded for emphasis. "Except when he wanted something from you. Boy, could he be a charmer. He'd turn up that accent of his and that smile, and it was almost impossible to say no to him."

Now that sounds like John, Gabi thought.

"The two of them were a terror." Megan shook her head, chuckling at memories. "They used to get into so much trouble, getting into things they shouldn't. But the worst was when our great-uncle came to live with us. It was a well-known family secret that Uncle Sean had escaped from

Northern Ireland after the police were able to trace several IRA bombings back to him. Uncle Sean knew all about explosives, and he taught some of what he knew to Connor and Liam."

Gabi felt her pulse rate pick up. "What kind of things?"

"Well, for one, he taught them how to use this putty-like stuff to create small explosions. Nothing dangerous. But Connor and Liam decided that the best thing to do was to use it to scare everyone in the neighborhood. They'd put it in garbage cans and then explode it when lots of people were passing by. Or, one time, during their last year in school together, they put it under a teacher's desk. And then, when she was at the blackboard with her back turned, they set it off. They caught so much grief for that, but they didn't care. I don't think they meant any harm by it, but still. Looking back on it now, it's a miracle no one ever got hurt."

"Did you, by any chance, tell any of this to the FBI?" Gabi asked. Her face felt hot, and she could actually feel her skin thumping to the beat of her pulse.

"No. I only spoke with them briefly, and honestly, I haven't thought about any of this in years. Not until now."

Gabi fidgeted, trying hard to stay still in order to let Megan sit with her memories. But she never was much good with being patient. "Why was it their last year in school together?"

Megan's smile faded. "It was terrible. Though back then, gang violence wasn't what it is today, when you've got lots of young men with little education and not a whole lot to do with their time, well… Liam's mother happened to be in the wrong place at the wrong time."

"Wow, that…"

"Sucks? Yeah, it did, and Liam was never the same after that. He was so angry. He blamed everyone in the neighborhood. I think he blamed the neighborhood itself, and the fact that most of us, our parents anyway, were poor immigrants. He stopped talking to Connor. He began studying all the time. The next year, he got himself into a private school in Manhattan on scholarship. Last I heard of him, he went off to college and changed his name. Beyond that, no one around our neighborhood ever heard from him again or knew what became of him."

Gabi's leg bounced rapidly. "Do you know what he changed his name to?"

"Nah. It was something generic though. Tom or Michael or something like that."

Gabi was leaning too far forward, and she noticed Megan pull back from her. "Could it have been John?"

Megan had folded her arms again. She glanced at her computer and shrugged. "Yeah, it's possible."

At that moment, a young man entered the room and snuck a quick peek in their direction. On catching sight of Megan, he ducked his head and lifted his hand to scratch the back of his neck before pushing through a second door on the other side of the office. Megan looked at her watch and frowned.

"Ms. Riley?" Gabi tried to bring the librarian's attention back to her, but Megan's attention had shifted to the door the young man had disappeared through.

Gabi glanced between the door and Megan. Gabi had long ago learned how the atmosphere changed when a sale had fallen through and when a potential customer wasn't listening anymore. Megan wasn't with Gabi anymore. Any hope of getting her back disappeared when the door opened and the young man reappeared, minus his backpack and baseball cap.

"You're late, Tyrone. Again."

"Yeah, sorry Ms. R. Fuh… Stupid subway didn't stop at my station."

"That's very interesting, Tyrone, since that marks the third time this month the train inexplicably passed your station."

Megan's sarcasm was lost on Tyrone. "You don't gotta tell me. Ask the fricking mayor about it." He pushed through the door that led into the library.

Megan's expression had returned to its earlier scowl, an expression Gabi thought looked at home on her. Whatever warmth the woman had exhibited reminiscing about her brother's younger years was gone. She huffed and turned her attention back to Gabi. "Ms. Feraru, I really must be getting back to work. You know the way out."

Gabi stood. "Thank you for your time, Ms. Riley." At the door, she paused. "Ms. Riley, how did your brother treat women? I mean, was he abusive to his girlfriends?"

Megan glanced up from her computer. "I assume you have a good reason for asking such a rude question. As far as I know, he treated them fine, but by the time he was dating, he and I didn't speak much anymore. I heard rumors that since they moved to Virginia, he hadn't been treating Deidre so nicely. But I never heard it from Deidre. Now, does that answer all your questions?"

"Yes, I think so." Gabi dug into her purse until she found the hot pink tiger striped card holder Sophia had given her for the holidays the previous year. "In case you remember Liam's new name, I'll leave you my card. It's got my work and cell numbers on it."

Megan wasn't paying any attention, so Gabi placed the card on the desk nearest to her and slipped back into the library.

16

DARKNESS GAVE way to gray as the train pulled out from beneath New York City's Penn Station. Since she'd descended into the subway after visiting Megan, the weather had taken a turn for the worse. The rain, for which most of the tri-state area had been waiting, was finally coming down in buckets.

Inside her purse, Elton John sang goodbye to the yellow brick road. He was cut off by the alert sound for a missed call. Gabi pulled her cell out and saw that Alina also had called fifteen minutes ago. She quickly hit the call back button and leaned back into the seat, legs stretched out in front of her. She watched the landscape blur by, absently tapping her fingers on the armrest.

"Gabi, where are you?"

"I was in the city. Why? You change your mind about the movies tonight?"

"Did you get any of my messages?"

Gabi heard tears in Alina's voice, and her fingers stilled. "No." *Amazing that a person's voice can break on such a short word,* Gabi thought. "What's happening?"

"I'm at Haven for Hope."

Gabi's dread turned to confusion. What was Alina doing at Haven for Hope?

"Mom and I moved Aunt Maggie here. About an hour ago."

Gabi didn't answer. She couldn't. Her mouth refused to form the shapes needed to speak. Numbness shot down her legs and through her arms, and though she couldn't feel her fingers anymore, she could tell that her grip on her phone was deathlike. She thought, for a moment, that she might faint.

"Did you hear what I said? Gabi? Oh no, I think I lost you. Gabi?"

"What the hell? Are you serious, Alina!" Gabi finally found her voice, eliciting several head snaps from the people in the seats around her. "Why would you do that? Who gave your mother permission to move my aunt?"

"She wouldn't wake up. I couldn't wake her up. The nurse couldn't wake her up. I didn't know what to do, and you weren't answering your cell." Alina paused. When she spoke again, her voice was less frantic and she spoke slowly. "Gabriella, Aunt Maggie is dying. I spoke to her oncologist, and he said there's nothing more they can do for her. He told you that apparently, but you didn't want to listen." Alina's voice sounded far away, and yet, Gabi could hear each word clearly. Each one was a pinprick of pain.

"It hasn't even been a full two months since she started her treatments. They need to give it more time." Gabi thought she might have been shouting.

In the seat in front of her, a woman in an intricately beaded blue and pink sari turned to look at her, one corner of her mouth tilted upward in a sympathetic half-smile. She reached her hand to touch Gabi, but Gabi rocked back, pulling away from her touch. The woman seemed to take no offence. She blinked slowly at Gabi before turning back around. Alina was saying something, but Gabi wasn't listening.

She tried to control her voice. "Stop talking, Alina. How did Monica even have the authority to move Aunt Maggie?"

"Aunt Maggie gave Mom co-power of attorney so that everything wouldn't fall on you. You didn't know?"

The day Gabi had met her friend BJ, when they were both fourteen years old, she'd rescued him from two bullies. In the process of protecting him, she'd been sucker punched by one of the older boys who'd cornered him in the gymnasium. She felt the same lack of air now as she'd felt then.

"I'll be in Cranford in half an hour. Wait for me at the hospice. I'm gonna talk to her doctors. Aunt Maggie promised me she'd fight this thing. She promised me."

"Gabi…" Alina's voice had softened. "I don't think Aunt Maggie intended to break her promise."

"Don't." Gabi's voice cracked, and she ended the call before her sister could respond.

It felt like a minute later when the conductor's voice, announcing Cranford train station, broke through her fog.

She hurried off the train, jogged to her car, a rental she'd been driving since her "accident," and peeled out of the parking lot. She managed to hit every red light on her way to the hospice, so it was twenty-five minutes later when she finally turned her engine off.

Instead of getting out of the car, she sat and stared at her mom's SUV. She'd bet anything this had been her mom's idea, moving Aunt Maggie. She could feel the blood rushing to her face, and she touched a hand to her cheek. It was hot. Angry tears gathered at the corners of her eyes, but she fought to hold them back. She grabbed her purse off the passenger seat, slammed the door behind her, and marched to the entrance.

"I'm here to see Maggie Oprea, and I'd like to speak to

whichever doctor has been assigned to her," she said before the smiling woman at the reception desk could utter a word. *Why do people smile in hospices,* she wondered. *It's rude.*

"Of course, dear," the woman replied, unfazed by Gabi's abrupt demand. She wore a fluffy pink sweater and a string of pearlescent beads around her neck.

Gabi bristled at the word dear.

"Her room number." Gabi tried to keep her voice in check.

The woman smiled again. "Room 236, dear. And I'll tell the doctor you'd like to speak to him."

Aunt Maggie was a small bundle of blankets in the middle of the twin bed when Gabi walked into the room. Alina was sitting in the chair next to the bed, rubbing her temples. There was a Haven for Hope pamphlet on her lap.

"Where's Monica?"

Alina looked up at Gabi, put the pamphlet on the table by the bed, and stood.

"Mom," she said, stressing the word, "went home."

"Her car is still here."

"I needed to borrow some folding chairs from her. It's easier to do with her car."

"You have folding chairs."

"I needed more. Remember? We're having a barbecue with some of Ryan's co-workers tomorrow."

"Oh, right, whatever. The doctor should be here any minute."

Alina bent over Aunt Maggie and straightened the blanket, then brushed a thin wisp of hair from her face. Her eyes glistening, she turned back to Gabi.

"What do you need to see the doctor for?" Alina kept her voice soft.

"We need to arrange her transfer to the hospital as soon

as possible." Gabi stepped toward Aunt Maggie. "Do they even still have her hooked up for chemo?"

"Stop, Gabriella." Alina placed herself in Gabi's way, hands in front of her, palms facing out.

"Stop what? The sooner she's at the hospital, the sooner she can start getting better again."

"She wasn't getting better, Gabi. She's not going to get better. She's dying, and the sooner you face that fact, the better."

"Uh-hmm. You asked to speak to me?" A man, likely in his early 60s, stood in the doorway. He had a short but thick black beard that was streaked with white, and he wore wire-rimmed glasses. Like the receptionist, he exuded a calm peacefulness Gabi found maddening.

"You're the doctor?"

"Yes, I'm Dr.—"

"I don't care what your name is."

"Gabriella! Dr. Singh, I apologize for my sister's behavior."

Gabi ignored Alina. "As I was saying, there seems to have been a misunderstanding. My aunt should not have been brought here. I'd like to make arrangements to have her transferred to the hospital right away. Also, if she's had her chemo port removed, please put it back."

Dr. Singh scanned the clipboard in his hands and blinked. When he looked back up at her, Gabi had to restrain herself from stepping forward to shake the look of calm compassion off of his face.

"Well?"

Gabi barely felt Alina's hand on her arm.

"Miss Feraru. I truly am sorry, but there has been no misunderstanding and no miscommunication. Your aunt's cancer has progressed too far. There's nothing the doctors at the hospital can do for her. Nothing the chemo can do except make her feel ill. Your aunt made this decision the last time she spoke with her doctor. Here, we can manage whatever pain she's in and keep her comfortable."

"I don't believe that for a second." Gabi rounded on her sister. "This was Monica's doing, wasn't it?"

Alina's voice, when she responded, was no longer soft. She stepped into the role of older sister taking charge, which always raised Gabi's defenses. "Enough, Gabriella. This is not the time or place for your recriminations against Mom. For God's sake, would you listen to the doctor?"

The doctor obviously decided to give them their privacy and left. Almost at the same time, Gabi's phone rang.

"Are you going to get that?"

Gabi was tempted to let it ring, just to piss off her sister. Instead, she stomped over to the chair she'd dropped her bag on and angrily pawed through it.

The phone displayed Violet's name.

"Violet, hi. Listen, this is a really bad time. Can I call you —" Gabi realized Violet was crying and tried to rein in her own anger. "What's wrong?"

"The police called. They've officially closed the case on George's death."

Gabi waited while Violet sobbed.

"They're calling it a suicide." Violet's voice dissolved into sobs.

"Gabi…" Alina stood looking at her. "Don't you have something more important to discuss than whatever that is right now?"

Gabi glanced at her sister, trying to process.

"Gabi, the detective told me they believe he overdosed on nitroglycerin because he felt guilty for killing Connor Foley." Violet started to sob again.

"Gabi." She heard the annoyance in Alina's voice.

"Gabi, I don't know what to do."

"Gabriella!" Her sister's annoyance was turning to anger.

"Gabi, please, you have to do something."

"Gabriella, get off the phone." She could see the tendons in her sister's neck.

If I hear my name one more time, I'm going to explode, Gabi thought.

"I have to go, Violet, but I promise I'll fix this. I'll fix everything." She hung up, leaving Violet in tears.

Alina was bent over the bed, murmuring to their aunt. "We're here, Aunt Maggie. We love you. It's okay," she said over and over.

"It's not okay. Nothing's okay." Gabi elbowed her sister aside, taking the most direct route to her aunt.

"Aunt Maggie, can you hear me? It's Gabi."

Aunt Maggie's eyelids fluttered open, though her dark-brown eyes didn't focus. "Gabi?"

Now on the other side of the bed, Alina watched, arms crossed in front of her chest, squeezing herself.

"I'm here. I'm here." Gabi slid her hand beneath the blankets to find Aunt Maggie's skeletal fingers. She was afraid to squeeze too hard.

"Where am I?"

Gabi leaned closer, lowering her voice so only her aunt could hear her. "Don't worry about that, Aunt Maggie. You're going to be fine. I'm going to take care of everything. You, and Major, and Connor, and everything. You just have to hold on for a little longer, okay?"

Aunt Maggie's eyes shut. Gabi leaned forward, kissed her on the forehead, and straightened up.

"What did you say to her?" Tears left beige streaks down Alina's cheeks.

Gabi wanted to tell her sister that it was none of her business, but she also didn't want to mess up their friendship.

They'd been estranged for so long, and she truly didn't want to go back to that. "Just that I love her."

Gabi looked back down at her aunt. *She looks so peaceful,* Gabi thought. The drugs she was on had taken away her fitfulness. Her hands didn't twitch anymore, and her face wasn't drawn tight from pain. For now, she'd let her aunt rest; she deserved the break. But Monday, it was off to the hospital, no matter what the doctors said.

A half hour later, while her aunt was still asleep, Gabi looked at her watch and realized she had to go. She had an important phone call to make. Plus, she should probably call Violet back to let her know she had a plan. "I have to go," Gabi said to her sister. "I have a dinner tomorrow night in the city that I need to prepare for. Are you going to stay here?"

"For a little while. I still have to go to the supermarket to pick up some things for tomorrow."

"Okay, call me if something happens. Otherwise, talk to you tomorrow."

It was mid afternoon the next day and Gabi had just pulled the side zipper up on her black satin pants when she heard the door slam downstairs.

"I don't have time for this," she mumbled, shrugging into a purple Old Navy fleece hoodie in case it was someone she didn't want to be half-naked in front of—though only a couple of close friends had a key to the house. From the sound of heels clicking on the stairs, Gabi knew Sophia was on her way up. The trailing sound of flip-flops probably came from Alina, though Alina was supposed to be at the hospice with Aunt Maggie, after Gabi had spent all of her morning there.

"Nice combo. Who knew satin and fleece go so well together?"

"Is that why you're here, to give me fashion advice?" Gabi pulled the hoodie back off and reached for a semi-attached sleeveless tank and velvet jacket. The turquoise sequence that adorned the front sparkled as she pulled it on. "Alina, aren't you supposed to be at the hospice?"

"I had to grab a few last-minute items for Ryan's barbeque. I dropped the stuff off at home and am heading to Haven for Hope now, but thought I'd stop by here first. What are you doing?"

"Getting ready for the SeaCirque dinner," Gabi answered, as if it should have been obvious. "What are the two of you doing here? Together?"

Sophia sat down on the edge of Gabi's bed, stroking the soft fleece sweatshirt. "Alina called me last night."

"Since when does Alina have your number?" Gabi asked, looking from one to the other. The two only knew each other through Gabi, and as far as Gabi knew, they weren't that close.

Sophia ignored Gabi's question. "Alina said you were having trouble accepting your aunt's prognosis."

Holding a necklace against her neck and checking in the mirror to see if it went with her outfit, Gabi leveled a glare at Alina's reflection. "I'm not having trouble accepting Aunt Maggie's prognosis. I'm the only one who seems to realize her death isn't inevitable. Not yet. She's barely begun to fight this. Just because Aunt Maggie thinks she's ready to give up doesn't mean she actually is. I know she's tired, but she'll get her second wind. She doesn't want to die. She told me so when the doctors first told her they suspected cancer. I'm going to see to it that she gets the chance to keep fighting."

Alina sighed. "Maybe you should skip this dinner. Stay

home with us and talk. Or go stay with Aunt Maggie and talk to her."

"About what, Alina? Huh? About how Aunt Maggie *is* dying and I have to accept that? Because if that's what it is, you can save your breath. I don't need to hear it."

"Fine, we can talk about whatever you want."

Gabi closed her eyes and let out a long breath before turning around to face Alina and Sophia. "Alina, I appreciate you wanting to talk. Really, I do. But I have to go to this dinner tonight. It's important."

Sophia looked intently at Gabi. "Why is it so important all of a sudden?" she asked, suspicion lacing her voice. "You're planning something, aren't you? What happened at the library yesterday? What are you up to?"

"Megan Riley confirmed our suspicions. And I'm going to confront John at tonight's dinner. I've already called Stefan and explained the whole thing to him. He's going to help me, and then we're going to call the FBI and turn John in. Then Major will be cleared of Connor's death, everyone will know John also killed Major, or if it was Brendan that killed him, that John was behind it and I'll be back here tomorrow to get Aunt Maggie into the hospital. Everything will go back to the way it was."

"You do realize how crazy that sounds, right?" Alina asked, throwing her hands in the air.

"And dangerous." Sophia had moved to the bedroom door. With her hand on the doorknob, she stood in the entrance as if she could block Gabi from leaving the room.

"I'll be fine. That's why I asked for Stefan's help. I may not like the guy, but he takes the reputation of SeaCirque seriously. He's not going to let John get away with murder and whatever else he's been doing."

"Why not call the FBI now? You can make sure they're there tonight so nothing can go wrong," Sophia said.

"And if they don't believe me? Or tell me not to go ahead with my plan? No, that would make it harder for me to get them to show up, even after we get John to confess."

"That makes absolutely no sense, Gabi," Alina said and exchanged a shared look of alarm with Sophia. "Please, slow down for a minute and think. You're rushing into this, and you're not thinking straight."

"Like I'm not thinking straight about Aunt Maggie, right? No, I know what I'm doing." Gabi put the finishing touches on her eyeshadow and looked from Alina to Sophia. Alina had her arms crossed over her chest with her I-know-what's-best-for-you mom face on. Sophia was still standing in the doorway, twisting the ring on her index finger, the corner of her eyes creased in concern. Gabi forced herself to take a deep breath, to lower her voice, and to slow her words. They were worried about her, and she shouldn't be angry at them for that. She needed them to understand.

"Maybe it does sound crazy. But I've thought it through, and I really do know what I'm doing. Trust me." Gabi looked from one to the other, holding eye contact until they both nodded. *Time to get out of here*, she thought—before they found a way to prevent her from leaving.

"I need to get going if I'm going to make it in time. You guys can stay here if you like. I'll talk to you tomorrow." She grabbed her phone, threw it in her clutch, and headed for the door. Sophia slowly moved out of Gabi's way, but not before exchanging another glance with Alina, who then nodded at Sophia.

"I'll walk down with you," Alina said, joining her at the top of the stairs. In her bedroom, Gabi could see Sophia picking her hoodie up off the bed and putting it on a hanger.

Gabi and Alina were quiet as they went down the stairs.

"Before our trip to Jamaica, I hadn't been in this house for, like, forever," Alina said softly.

"I know. Aunt Maggie was so happy when you started coming around." Gabi smiled at the memory of her aunt's grin the first time Alina had come for dinner.

"Me too. I'd forgotten how much I missed her and how she reminded me so much of Daddy."

Gabi and her sister paused at the door. Alina was biting the inside of her bottom lip, and Gabi was surprised to realize she was too.

Upstairs, she could hear Sophia talking, but she couldn't make out any words. *She's probably talking to herself about how stubborn I am,* Gabi thought.

"I missed you too, Gabi. I know we were never really close, but I missed you. Now that we're friends, I don't want to lose my only sister."

Gabi instinctively ducked her head to avoid the fear in Alina's eyes. "You're not going to lose me, Alina. I promise. I've got this under control. Once tonight is over, everything is going to be okay again."

17

GABI BARELY NOTICED the smartly dressed doorman holding the door open for her as she entered the Waldorf Astoria. She felt separate from the world around her, though each gust of wind against her skin had felt like a gale. The sun had been going down behind the buildings when she'd walked from the lot she'd parked in, and it had never looked more vibrant. Without thinking, Gabi let her feet follow the signs directing guests to Ballroom B for the SeaCirque dinner.

In the elevator, Gabi fingered Agent Jacks's business card, which she'd tucked into her evening purse before she left the house. It would be easy to call him for help. *What's wrong with a little backup?* she thought. But she and Stefan had agreed it would be best to get John to confess to them first and then detain him until the police got there.

The door opened to a sea of cocktail dresses, ball gowns, and tuxedos. The sight of so much glitter soothed her fears. Nothing bad could happen among so much glamour, Sophia would have said.

She had arranged with Stefan to confront John after

dinner, after the first round of speeches. Gabi checked her phone for the time. Forty-five minutes or so until dinner. She wound her way through the crowds, stopping at one of the small bars to get herself a drink. Never a wine drinker, she had expected to order a beer and was pleasantly surprised that she was able to get a Bellini.

"Gabi, right?" A vaguely familiar man stood to her right.

"Yes," she said aloud, while thinking to herself, *What kind of douche wears dark sunglasses to a fancy banquet?*

The man saw the confusion on her face and smiled. "Bob." He held out his hand. "We met on the *Sea Fantasy*."

Gabi didn't remember meeting him, but Jill had introduced her to several people over the course of the cruise. "Oh, right. Nice to see you again. How has your summer been?"

The corners of Bob's eyes crinkled as he smiled. "You don't remember me, do you?"

Her first instinct was to deny his friendly accusation, but it was clear he'd already caught on to her. "No, I don't. I'm sorry. And I'm usually pretty good at putting names to faces."

"Well, Bob is a pretty generic name, but no one has ever told me I have a forgettable face before."

"*What?* No, I didn't mean that." Gabi stammered for a moment until she realized he was joking. "You do look familiar though."

"That's okay. I'm used to it. Pretty women never seem to remember me."

Gabi looked more closely at him, and her memory stirred. She doubted his claim and was surprised she couldn't place him. With his high cheekbones and mussed-up black hair, Bob was quite attractive. An image of him in a suit, hand outstretched as if to shake hands, suddenly came to mind. *Aha,* she thought. *They must have met the night of the inaugural when everyone was dressed up.*

She was on the verge of flirting back when she spotted John chatting with a group of people not too far away. Seeing him brought back her main reason for being at the dinner. It wiped any thoughts of flirtation from her mind.

She took a sip from the bellini the bartender had handed her then put it down on the bar. "I'm so sorry, Bob, but I need to find my table. If you'll excuse me. It was nice meeting you again."

The humor faded from his eyes, and for a moment, Gabi thought she saw worry flash across his features, but she quickly dismissed the idea. Why would Bob be worried about her?

"Of course. I look forward to seeing you again soon," he said. She saw her reflection in his dark glasses as he looked directly into her eyes. Slightly flustered by the attention and also preoccupied by her night's mission, Gabi mumbled a quick goodbye and practically speed-walked away.

He must think I'm a freak, she thought as she looked for her assigned table. Others were doing the same. She spotted table eight and quickly located her place card. The setting next to hers was reserved for Elaine, but Gabi was pretty sure her boss wouldn't be showing up. She sat down after first looping her purse over the chair back and then scanned the room again for Stefan and John.

John was still working the room, this time chatting with two older women, both of whom seemed utterly charmed by him. After a second sweep of the space, Gabi spotted Stefan in the corner of the ballroom speaking with Carl Stegner, the CEO of SeaCirque Cruise Line. She briefly wondered if Stefan had clued him in on what was happening, but judging from their relaxed postures, she doubted it.

Then her line of sight to the two men was blocked as two women sat down.

"Hilda Shaw," said the first, holding out her hand, the

polish on her perfectly manicured nails matching the dark-red power suit she wore.

"Greta Shaw," said the second, her handshake as firm as her sister's. She wore a steel gray pants suit, and opalescent pearls were her only display of vanity.

Gabi knew of the Shaw sisters by reputation only. They consistently won awards for top producers for most of the cruise lines and even some of the tour operators.

"Gabi Feraru," she replied, half standing to shake each woman's hand.

"Any idea what the announcement is going to be?" Hilda asked.

"No idea," Gabi said, vaguely remembering the postcard invitation had said something about a big announcement.

"Perhaps they're building another ship," Greta said.

Gabi sipped at her water glass, watching as the two sisters argued over the possibility of a new ship, what was going to be served for dinner, and which cruise line hosted the best events.

"I believe this is my seat," a voice said to her right, and Gabi swallowed an expletive.

"Sophia! What the—" She glanced at the Shaw sisters, who had stopped their own argument and were looking at her and Sophia with interest. "What are you doing here?" Gabi whispered fiercely and grabbed Sophia's arm to pull her into the empty chair.

"Ow, geez. A bit tense, huh?" Sophia rolled her eyes at Gabi's silent glare. "Fine. After you left, I called Elaine and told her what was going on. She told me to take her spot so I can keep an eye on you."

"I knew I heard you talking to someone when I was leaving. I should have known you were up to something."

Sophia mumbled something under her breath that sounded like "half of it."

"What did you say?"

"Nothing. I'm just mumbling about how pigheaded you are."

"Me? I told you to let me deal with it. You're just as stubborn as I am."

"I don't deny that." Sophia lowered her voice so that it came out more as a hiss than a whisper. "Given a choice between letting you face a killer by yourself and risking our friendship by ignoring your royal decree, I chose to be here. Deal with it."

As they'd been whispering at each other, a tall Black woman in a lightly sequined black and gold cocktail dress had approached the podium and was now clearing her throat, trying to get the crowd's attention.

In response, the Shaw sisters began tapping their wine glasses with their knives to help.

"Don't get in my way," Gabi whispered out of the side of her mouth as she straightened in her chair and turned her attention to the stage. Out of the corner of her eye, she could see Sophia's triumphant smirk.

"Good evening, ladies and gentlemen," the woman on stage said. "I believe most of you know me, but for those who don't, I'm Behia Hughley, executive vice president of marketing at SeaCirque Cruise Line. Welcome to the Waldorf Astoria. I know you are all wondering what our big announcement is. I've heard so many rumors bandied about that my head is spinning. But I have to tell you, my favorite is that we've decided to enter the space travel market and are designing a space cruise ship."

She paused to let the crowd chuckle. "I can tell you with absolute surety, SeaCirque is sticking to the oceans and will leave space to Richard Branson and Elon Musk."

A second round of laughter swept the crowd.

"Tonight's announcement is sadly somewhat bittersweet

and in care of our executive vice president of sales Stefan Davidson."

Gabi choked on the water she'd been sipping and snapped her head up to look first at Behia and then at Stefan, who was waiting by the stage stairs. Was he going to tell the audience what was going on? She scanned the crowd, looking for John. What if he ran when Stefan said something? They'd never catch him. Gabi finally located John at a table one row back and to the right. He looked unaffected by Behia's comment and didn't seem nervous in the least.

"Without further ado, let's get Stefan up here."

Behia finished speaking, and Stefan walked solemnly up the steps, gave Behia a quick peck on the cheek, and turned to face his audience.

"Good evening, my friends. Thank you for joining me for this special dinner." Stefan paused, and Gabi couldn't decide if it was for dramatic impact, or if he was hesitant to continue with his speech.

"I have been with SeaCirque Cruise Line for thirty-two years, and in that time, I've seen this cruise line grow from three ships to seventeen. With your help, I've watched SeaCirque go from a barely known entity in the cruise industry to one of the most widely known cruise brands in the world. I'm grateful for all the work you have done on our behalf and proud of the blood, sweat, and tears I've given this cruise line. In three days, I will turn sixty-five years old." Stefan paused and took a sip of water from a glass that was sitting on the podium.

"Ohhh," one of the Shaw sisters whispered, echoing the soft murmur that was slowly spreading around the room.

"I can tell from the looks on most of your faces, you already know what's coming next," Stefan continued. "At the end of this year, I will hang up my executive stripes and join the ranks of the retired."

The murmur in the audience magnified. Gabi was as surprised as everyone else.

"Please, please. You'll have all of dinner to talk," Stefan said, and the buzz quieted. "It has been the highlight of my life to work for SeaCirque and help it grow. I, of course, intend to check in from time to time to make sure my successor is keeping up the good work." He smiled when the mention of his successor ignited a renewed flurry of whispers.

"That announcement will come later, so you have all dinner to mull it over. And I expect a few betting pools might even get started," he joked.

"How does he expect to confront John during dinner, hand him over to the FBI, and then get back up on stage to calmly announce his successor as if nothing had happened?" Sophia whispered in Gabi's ear.

"Shh," Gabi warned, eyeing the others at the table to be sure no one had overheard. But everyone's attention was still focused on Stefan. "I don't know. I really don't." Gabi could feel the pulse in her throat throbbing. Was Stefan backing out of their plan? Maybe she should call the FBI and let them handle it.

On stage, Stefan was finishing up. "Bon appétit. I'll be back to talk to you again later." He exited the stage, stopping at several tables to shake hands and kiss cheeks, slowly making his way toward Gabi's table.

"Stefan dear, I can't believe you're leaving us," Hilda Shaw cried, swooshing up from her seat to hug him.

"Yes, Stefan, how can you leave? You will miss us terribly," Greta Shaw said.

In spite of her shock at Stefan's announcement, Sophia managed an eye roll at the Shaw sisters' theatrics. But Gabi's surprise, and sickening fear that she was going to be on her own with John, dampened her appreciation of the moment.

"Ah ladies, you are, of course, right. I will miss both of you terribly," he said, giving Hilda a one-armed squeeze.

"Um, Stefan," Gabi interrupted.

With his arm now around Greta, Stefan turned to Gabi briefly. "Ah Gabi, I think I can guess what you're thinking, but I promise I will see to everything that needs to be addressed before I leave."

"Yes, but—"

Stephan's single cocked eyebrow stopped Gabi. He released Greta from his embrace and kissed her hand.

When he finally extracted himself from the sisters, he pressed a hand into Gabi's shoulder. "You have my word," he said, bending to kiss her on the cheek as if thanking her for her well-wishes. But he left his mouth by her ear for a moment longer. "All of this unpleasantness will be over by the end of the night. You have my word."

As he spoke, the hairs on her arm stood up straight and a chill raced its way up her spine.

"Look, Hilda dear, she's blushing," Greta Shaw said to her sister, mistaking Gabi's flushed face for embarrassment.

"What did Stefan say?" Sophia whispered.

"He said he was going to take care of everything."

"That's it? That's all he said?"

Gabi nodded, and before she could say more, the man on her left tapped her on the hand and asked if she could pass the butter. As she did so, her own stomach rumbled, the hunger momentarily displacing the disquiet in her mind. She snagged a butter ball for herself before passing the dish and selected a roll from the breadbasket.

"Who do you think will replace Stefan?" the butter requester asked both Gabi and Sophia.

"I haven't got a clue," Gabi answered. "I'd love it if they promoted Jill Vega, because she's my sales rep. And the best rep I have with any of the cruise lines I work with."

The entrée was served shortly afterwards, and the table ate and chatted, waiting for Behia to return to the podium. The waiters circled the room to collect dirty dishes and bring out dessert. As the young man who had been serving their table all night leaned over to take Gabi's dinner plate, he handed her a folded piece of paper.

"I was instructed to give this to you, ma'am," he said.

The chicken that only moments ago she'd thoroughly enjoyed the taste of suddenly sat leaden in her stomach. She waited for the waiter to leave the table then unfolded the paper with fingers that weren't normally so clumsy. *Meet me in the Bourbon Street Boardroom at 8:15. Stefan*

Gabi felt the blood draining from her face. It was really happening.

"Gabi, what's wrong? You look sick," Sophia said.

Gabi handed the note to Sophia.

"Oh." She cleared her throat. "Are you really sure you should go through with this?"

"I have to. Even if it turns out Brendan actually killed Connor, it all comes down to John. He started it. It's time to finish it," Gabi replied.

"At least call that FBI guy or the police before you meet him." Sophia's face was white and Gabi could feel the fear radiating off of her.

"Relax. I'll have Stefan with me. We'll be okay." Gabi wasn't sure who she was trying to calm down, Sophia or herself.

"In a boardroom? Where no one can see you?"

"Makes sense to me to have a talk like that in a private location where no one can accidentally overhear us. Plus, if Stefan stands by the door, he can stop John from bolting."

"I don't know, Gabs. It seems weird."

"It'll be fine. We'll confront John. Get him to admit he's the one who brought Connor in on this. Maybe he'll even admit to killing Connor and Major. And then it'll all be over."

Gabi didn't know if she was picking up on Sophia's fear, but the nagging uneasiness she'd felt earlier in the evening returned. She looked at her watch, which read 8:07. She tried to pass the time chatting and picking at her fruit tart, but every bite turned sour in her stomach.

"Gabi, I really, really think this is a bad idea. Please."

Sophia's nervousness annoyed Gabi. "It'll be fine," she snapped and glanced at her watch again. It was 8:10. "I better get going."

"You'll be too early," Sophia said a bit too loudly, grabbing Gabi's arm.

"Is everything all right, dears?" Hilda Shaw asked. All eyes at the table were on Gabi and Sophia.

"Yes, of course. I just have—" Gabi paused, trying to think of something to say "—a quick phone appointment. And I didn't want to disturb the table with the conversation."

Greta Shaw raised an eyebrow, glancing at Sophia's hand still on Gabi's arm.

"Right." Sophia cleared her throat. "You see, the client is on West Coast time, and Gabi isn't supposed to call until five-thirty his time." She finished weakly. "It's too early."

The two sisters looked at each other. Each shrugged a shoulder, mirroring the other's skepticism. Conversation resumed, and Gabi quickly darted from the table. Sophia followed closely on her heels.

18

____

"Wʜᴀᴛ ᴀʀᴇ ʏᴏᴜ ᴅᴏɪɴɢ?" Gabi hissed at Sophia as her best friend rose to follow her.

"I'm coming with you."

"No, you're not."

Sophia pulled hard on Gabi's arm, half turning Gabi to face her.

"Listen. Maybe you're right. Maybe you'll meet up with Stefan, confront John, somehow get him to admit everything without him then running away, and then we'll go back to the table. But even if that's the case, you're my best friend, and I'm not letting you go alone. Period. Got it?"

Gabi wanted to argue with Sophia, but she recognized the look on Sophia's face. She wasn't going to give in, and Gabi knew there was no point in trying to fight it.

"Okay. Okay. We go together. Alright?"

"It'd be more alright if we went back to the table and let the police handle everything."

"Sophia." Gabi said her friend's name, using the same tone of voice she used when warning her nephews not to touch something they knew was off-limits.

"Just kidding," Sophia replied, though it was clear she was anything but. Too much of the white in Sophia's eyes was showing, and Gabi could clearly see how uncomfortable her friend was. Before Sophia's fear could weaken her own resolve, Gabi headed toward the hallway where all the meeting rooms were located.

"Let's go. I'm pretty sure the boardroom is this way. You coming or not?" They turned the corner, passed the men's restroom, and found themselves in front of a door with the words Bourbon Street written on it. Inside, Gabi could hear men's voices.

"This must be it," whispered Gabi. "But I hear more than one person in there. I thought Stefan and I were meeting first, before confronting John."

"Maybe Stefan is the one being rational and has the police in there with him."

Gabi didn't appreciate the sarcasm in Sophia's voice. "There's only one way to find out." She pushed open the door and almost tripped when she saw Stefan talking to John. At the same time, her cell phone beeped, alerting her to a text message. Her uneasiness returned with a vengeance. She almost turned around, but Sophia was so close behind her, it forced her into the room. It was too late to back out.

Crap. What was John doing here? They were supposed to go over the game plan first. What if John reacted violently? Suddenly, she didn't feel as prepared as she'd thought she was. Her phone beeped again.

"Just ignore it," Sophia said, her bright-blue eyes flashing in panic as she glanced from the men to the door they'd passed through. "What's he doing here?" she hissed in a whisper.

Maybe it was the timing, seeing John's confusion at the same moment her phone beeped, but Gabi felt sure she was receiving an urgent message on her phone. Ignoring Sophia's question and Stefan's look of impatience as he waited for them to step farther inside, Gabi pulled her phone out of her clutch and hit the read button. Nausea hit her like a fist, and she grunted, grabbing on to Sophia to steady herself.

Sophia glanced at Gabi and at the look in her eyes. Sophia tried to ask what had startled her, but though her mouth formed shapes, she made no sound. Gabi shook her head helplessly. It was too late; Stefan was already headed over. He had his hand on John's shoulder and was guiding him towards them.

Gabi swallowed hard, almost choking on the acrid saliva in her mouth. She pulled Sophia hard behind her and turned to face Stefan. She knew her eyes were too wide, that her hands were already trembling. Try as she might, she couldn't stop the panic that was racing through her body. She inhaled sharply through her nose and tried to forced herself to let it out as slowly as possible.

Only a few steps away, Stefan zeroed in on Gabi's face, and time stopped. He studied the look in her eyes, and she saw the moment realization hit. Then, as quickly as time had slowed down, it hit fast forward and Stefan lunged toward Gabi.

John glanced from Stefan to Gabi as he was pulled forward, confusion and annoyance plain on his face. Gabi noticed that Stefan's formerly guiding hand now firmly gripped John's upper arm.

"Aye, Stefan, watch it." John tried to pull his arm free.

In the space between blinks, Stefan whipped out a small revolver from his waistband and slammed the butt into John's temple. Stefan's eyes never strayed from Gabi's face as John crumpled to the floor.

One side of Stefan's mouth inched up, and with his lips pressed together, he shook his head at Gabi.

Gabi whimpered in response, unable to stop the sound

from forcing its way past her clenched throat muscles. Next to her, she could hear similar sounds coming from Sophia.

"I was really hoping to avoid all this ugliness." Stefan pointed the gun, a tiny thing that almost looked like a toy, at Gabi and Sophia.

Sophia giggled involuntarily at the sight of the small gun but strangled the laugh into a cough.

Stefan gave them another half smile. "Believe me, it won't be so funny when the punch this little micro-pistol packs tears through your body."

It was Sophia's turn to whimper, and Gabi grabbed her hand, her own fear constricting her fingers into a tight squeeze. "I need a Band-Aid," Sophia moaned.

The absurdity of Sophia's comment barely registered in Gabi's mind as her gaze remained locked on the gun in front of her.

Stefan was put off by Sophia's request, and for the tiniest second, the hand holding the gun wavered. But he quickly recovered and jerked the gun from side to side, ushering them farther into the meeting room and away from the door. Bending down, he grabbed the neck of John's jacket, and without taking the gun off of the women, he dragged John backwards.

"I truly thought this could be avoided," he said, the effort of dragging John with one hand mingling with regret and blame in his voice. "But, no, you had to keep pushing. In the corner, next to those extra chairs," he directed. "You should have paid attention to my message to back off."

"*You're* the one who left that message?"

Stefan ignored Gabi. "It turned out not to matter. Honestly, this was better. You thought it was John. 'All the evidence pointed to him,' you said." He paused, his eyes narrowed as he looked at her. "So I made it so. All your imaginary evidence is now actually there. It was perfect. We confront John with our evidence," he said, stressing the last word, "and turn him in. By the time any doubts arose, I'd be long gone." He paused again, his eyes unfocused, perhaps staring into a future he imagined for himself.

John groaned, snapping Stefan out of his reverie. His eyes narrowed even more, and Sophia's hand spastically squeezed Gabi's at the look in his eyes.

He turned to face them again. "It was a done deal," he growled at Gabi. "What happened? An hour ago, you were still convinced it was John." Stefan twitched as he noticed the phone still in Gabi's hand. "That text message. What was it?"

"It was Megan Riley."

Stefan showed no sign of recognizing the name.

"You knew her as Megan Foley. She knew you had changed your name but couldn't remember what it was when I saw her. She just remembered."

Stefan's face blanched. "Megan? You spoke to Connor's sister? Fuck. You're something else."

Gabi had never heard so much venom in Stefan's voice before. He was always as highbrow as they come, so his dive into vulgarity hammered home the danger they were in. How much danger she'd put them in.

"Megan knows the whole truth," Gabi said desperately, trying to appeal to whatever common sense Stefan still had. "If you kill us, she'll know."

"Kill you?" Stefan shook his head, his lips stretched into a smile. "I'm not going to kill you."

Gabi's knees almost buckled in relief.

"John is going to do that." Stefan nudged the semi-conscious man with the toe of his shoe. John groaned, and Sophia moaned in fear.

"A Band-Aid. I really need a Band-Aid," she said, more loudly than the small room called for.

"A Band-Aid?" Stefan's surprised laugh sounded genuine. "I don't think a Band-Aid is going to help you now."

Gabi was afraid Sophia was on the verge of losing it. After all, she could feel her own panic trying to upend her last remaining shred of sanity. All she could think to do was keep Stefan talking. "I don't get it though. Why kill Connor? Seems to me you and he had a good thing going. Why stop it?"

"We did have a good thing going. But Connor thought he owned me because of it. Thought he could tell me what to do. That retirement announcement…" He waved his hand in the general direction of the ballroom. "That was for real."

Stefan stopped speaking, and for a moment his body sagged. "I'm tired. I've had enough. I've got plenty of money to get me through a nice retirement someplace tropical. And Connor had made out almost as well."

Saying Connor's name brought back all Stefan's anger. "But Connor, he was always a little bit too greedy. He never understood the concept of moderation. He always had to have more, do more, push harder. I told him I was done. The partnership was over. But he wouldn't accept it. Said he'd tell everyone if I backed out. That I'd blackmailed him into it. Hah. Like anyone'd believe it. Plus, that brother-in-law of his was starting to nose around. He wanted in on whatever Connor had going. I couldn't take any chances. And anyway, who's going to miss Connor?"

"What about Major? Lots of people miss Major," Gabi said.

"I tried to get Major to back down," Stefan said, practically spitting. "But he was a crazed bulldog, just like you. Wouldn't let go of it, no matter how many times I told him there was nothing there. 'Retire, let it go, enjoy life with your wife,' I told him. I didn't want to kill him, but he gave me no choice. It was so easy to mix a bunch of nitro into his food.

And now…" Stefan's breath came hard and fast, his eyes laser focused on Gabi and Sophia, who both watched as he pulled himself together. He slowed his breathing and forced his shoulders down. "And now, poor, innocent John here has to kill you ladies and then kill himself in remorse. All because *you* wouldn't back down."

"Band-Aid. Band-Aid. I really need a Band-Aid," Sophia yelled, tears pouring down her face.

"Would you shut up about your stupid Band-Aid," Stefan yelled back, swinging the gun around to point at her directly.

Without thinking, Gabi stepped in front of Sophia. "Please, Stefan, you don't—"

The storage room door burst open. "FBI!"

Stefan recoiled, and for a fraction of a second, his gaze locked with Gabi's. Surprise and rage were laid bare. Then a bright flash filled her vision, and she felt her body twist sideways. Pain became the focal point of all her senses.

19

For the umpteenth time that day, Gabi blinked her eyes in rapid succession and tried to focus on something other than the ache in her chest. She wanted desperately to leave, to walk out into the sweltering August afternoon and leave the suffocation of sitting shiva in her mother's house behind. It was too warm inside, too full of bad memories and, currently, too full of people forcing their condolences onto her. The soft pats on the back of her hand and the coarse rub of dry lips kissing her cheek made her more nauseous with each passing moment. But she'd never hear the end of it if she left—not from Monica, not from Alina, not from Sophia.

And what was there to run away to anyway? All that was left was Aunt Maggie's empty house. Well, Gabi's empty house now. Aunt Maggie had left it to her in her will. Gabi swallowed a sob that threatened to force its way out and blinked her eyes again. *Don't think about it,* she told herself. *Push it away, push it down. Not here in front of all these people.*

"Gabi, can you grab the extra plate of cheese in the fridge?" Alina asked from the doorway of the kitchen. "I promise you can retreat back in here after you help me refill the serving platters. I swear a bunch of Jewish mourners eat enough to feed my family for a week."

"But they bring enough meatloaf and brisket to make up for it," Sophia said, swooping into the kitchen with a tinfoil-wrapped dish balanced on one hand and holding a fruit basket with the other. "This"—she indicated the dish with her chin—"is from cousin Sheila, and this"—she nodded to the basket—"is from someone who said he was Tom or Jim, or maybe it was Roger. He said he knows your mom."

The challenge of finding space in her mother's already too-full refrigerator for yet another dish that "just needs to be popped into the oven" helped pull Gabi from the brink of tears.

"Put those on the counter," she directed Sophia. "And can you take this into the other room and help Alina?"

"Didn't she ask you to help?" Sophia chided.

"I've only got one working arm," Gabi said, nodding down to her right arm, which rested in a sling.

"You only need one arm to carry a platter of cheese," Sophia said.

"Please, Soph, I can't."

"Hey, I'm messing with you." Sophia took Gabi's free hand and squeezed it. "It's okay. You don't have to go out there right now. Take your time."

"Thanks," Gabi said, again feeling the hotness of unshed tears burning her eyes.

After Sophia had left, Gabi turned back to the fridge and began reorganizing shelves, yet again, to open up some more space. Thankfully, the items in the fruit basket didn't need to be kept cold. Seeing some space at the very back of the fridge, she tried to shove one of the Pyrex containers farther back to open up room in front of it, but it refused to budge. Something was wedged behind it, preventing it from going farther. She pulled the container out to grab whatever was in the way. It was a glass jar of Gray Poupon lying on its side, crusted mustard visible around the edges.

This time Gabi couldn't stop the sob from ripping through her body. She hated the stuff, but it had been Aunt Maggie's favorite.

Gabi sat on the floor, the bottle of mustard cradled in her hand, and cried. Aunt Maggie had died the night Gabi had been shot. She'd never gotten a chance to say goodbye. Her lungs ached as she tried to catch her breath between sobs. All she could feel was a molten-hot pain in her chest.

Arms wrapped around her.

"Oh, Gabs, it's okay. Let it out. I've got you." It was Sophia's voice, and Gabi leaned into her.

"I wasn't there," she sobbed. "I wasn't with her at the end. I left her alone. I should have been there. I should have told her I loved her. What if her last thoughts were that I was angry at her?"

Gabi couldn't speak anymore. She could barely breathe. She wished she could reach her hands inside herself and rip out her heart so it wouldn't hurt anymore.

"Oh, Gabi. Aunt Maggie knew you loved her. And she was asleep when she passed. It was peaceful."

"What if you're wrong?"

Sophia took Gabi's face and turned it so Gabi was looking into Sophia's eyes. "Gabi, Aunt Maggie knew how much you loved her. And she loved you. Fiercely."

Gabi searched Sophia's face and found the truth. Though Gabi and Aunt Maggie had told each other they loved each other all the time, the words had never truly been needed. They both knew it, and Gabi's temper tantrum at the end wouldn't have changed that.

It still hurt, knowing she'd never see Aunt Maggie again. Never get to laugh at their inside jokes or sit in companionable silence as they both read on a rainy evening. It still hurt, but the sharp pain inside her chest had eased enough for her to pull away from Sophia and wipe her eyes.

"Your blouse. I got mascara all over it."

Sophia smiled sadly. "I've got another one in my bag. I figured there'd be lots of crying. You okay?"

Gabi nodded. "Yeah, go on. I just need a moment."

Sophia hugged Gabi. Gabi could see that Sophia was holding back her own tears as she left to find her spare blouse.

A little while later, she became aware of pins and needles forming along her foot. The cold bottle of mustard had sweated into her silk top, and the chilly air from the open refrigerator door cooled the tears on her cheeks. She gently put the Gray Poupon back in the fridge on one of the door ledges and shoved the two baked lasagnas or briskets or whatever they were into the fridge.

As she closed the door, not sure what she should do next, someone cleared their voice behind her. A deep, soft voice intruded on her thoughts. "Miss Feraru, please allow me to offer my sincerest condolences."

Gabi turned around, bracing herself to politely accept the sympathies—and probably another fruit basket—from someone she didn't really know. What she wasn't prepared for was FBI Agent Jacks.

"Agent Jacks. What are you doing here?" Gabi startled, and the throbbing in her shoulder flared up. The dull ache was a welcome relief from the hotter pain she didn't know what to do with.

It had been only five days since the night she'd last seen Agent Jacks. At the time, a bullet was lodged in her shoulder, Stefan was lifeless on the floor, and Sophia was ashen faced, asking her over and over again if she was okay. The rest of that night, from the moment Agent Jacks burst through the door and Stefan's gun went off as his body stiffened in surprise, enough to make his finger squeeze the trigger, remained a blur for Gabi. She remembered someone barking questions at her and Agent Jacks telling that someone to back off. She didn't remember answering questions and didn't remember leaving the boardroom or getting to the hospital. She thought she vaguely remembered flashing lights and a siren.

Mostly she remembered the look of surprise on Stefan's face and the emptiness in his eyes as his body lay on the floor. She still saw his vacant face when she wasn't expecting it—like when she was brushing her teeth or slipping into sleep at night. Had Aunt Maggie had that look on her face when the nurse found her while Gabi was being rushed to the hospital? Had she been surprised in the moment she died? Was she lonely? Disappointed that Gabi wasn't with her?

But then Sophia's words came back to her, stilling the questions. She believed that Aunt Maggie was at peace when she died. It had been nothing at all like Stefan's death.

"I thought you'd want to know that we found everything we needed on Mr. Davidson's computer and cell phone," Agent Jacks said. "All his files, the texts between him and Mr. Foley. His bank account. The FBI has officially cleared Mr. Thomas of any wrongdoing."

Her surprise at his sudden presence, the resurgence of the pain in her shoulder, and her own embarrassment at being caught with makeup smeared across her face and tear-soaked hair got the better of her. "And you thought today," she bit out, pointing her chin in the direction of the mourners murmuring in small groups, "was a good time to fill me in."

Agent Jacks flinched, and Gabi immediately regretted the harshness of her response.

"I heard about your aunt. I wanted to offer my condolences. And to see how you were doing." He indicated her shoulder. "I figure getting shot isn't a regular occurrence for a travel agent."

"Advisor." Her corrective response was automatic. The words were out of her mouth before she could even think.

"Right, travel advisor. As I said, I wanted to let you know everything has been settled. And I wanted to offer my condolences to you and your family. I'm glad to see you're up and about and doing okay. I won't take up any more of your time."

"I'm sorry, Agent Jacks. That was uncalled for of me. Please, can you tell me what was really going on?"

"Of course. Would you like to go for a walk? It doesn't take a detective to see that you need a break from all this," he said.

Once they'd exited the house, Agent Jacks began telling Gabi what the FBI had managed to piece together.

"Stefan Davidson's real name was Liam Mulrooney. He and Connor had known each other as children. But you had figured all that out already?"

"I knew about Liam, but I didn't know Stefan was Liam until…until it was too late," Gabi said, indicating her shoulder.

"Perhaps if you'd let us know what you knew…" Agent Jacks left the sentence unfinished. "But I digress. Liam, or Stefan as you knew him, was incredibly intelligent and very good at a lot of things."

"Like explosives, apparently," Gabi interrupted.

"Like plastic explosives. But more importantly, he was very skilled at computer programming. He's been with SeaCirque from almost the beginning and, in the early days, had a hand in writing the code for the booking system. He built a back door that let him create false bookings that triggered commission payments. None of the commission payments were so large that anyone would really notice, but over the years, they added up. He worked with hand-selected agents—er, advisors—to create real bookings to fill the rooms needed for the fake bookings."

"But Connor's only been around for a few years. And what about all the times the booking system was updated? Stefan was a senior executive, so he wouldn't have been writing code anymore," Gabi asked.

"You really would be a great detective, Gabi," Agent Jacks said. "You're right. Before Connor, there were at least five other travel advisors, spread out across the country, that Stefan involved in his scheme. Each one was forced out after a certain number of years, and until Connor, none of them objected."

"And the booking engine?"

"Sadly, money can get lots of people to break the law. Stefan always had an inside guy in the IT department to create and maintain his back door. Those inside guys didn't fare as well as the advisors he worked with. When we started digging, we realized at least three former IT employees of SeaCirque met unusual ends."

Gabi pulled up short. "So, Connor wasn't even the first?"

"No, it doesn't look like it."

Agent Jacks was quiet for a moment, but Gabi could see him side-eyeing her, as if weighing whether to continue talking.

"Was there something else?" she asked.

Agent Jacks inhaled deeply before responding. "We think Stefan may have been responsible for your car accident. After Sophia told me about the incident, I reached out to your mechanic. He told me the brake line had been nicked. While that's something that can happen on its own —say you drove over some debris on the road—that's unlikely. The small nick would have allowed the fluid to drip out slowly so you wouldn't notice until it was too late. Unless there's someone else that's got it in for you, the most likely scenario is that Stefan did it. Or, probably, paid someone else to do it."

Gabi had stopped walking when Agent Jacks revealed the news of the nicked brake line. It was one thing to suspect her accident had been deliberate. It was something else entirely to know for sure.

"Are you okay? Would you like to head back to the house?"

Gabi stood still for a moment, looking at the slowly darkening sky, trying to process everything Agent Jacks had told her about what had been going on at SeaCirque all these years, that no one, until Major, had ever noticed. He must have felt so alone, she thought. If only he'd said something to her. Would she have been able to help? Would she even have believed him?

"It's all so crazy," she said, finally looking at Agent Jacks. And, in that moment, as the light of the sunset silhouetted him from behind, something else clicked. "You're Bob," she blurted out. "The guy wearing the sunglasses at the dinner."

Agent Jacks chuckled, and like the first time she'd ever seen him on the cruise ship and then again at the dinner, Gabi couldn't help but notice how attractive he really was.

"I can't believe I fell for the Superman/Clark Kent glasses thing," she said.

"I was so sure you'd see right through my disguise," he said as they started to walk again. "But you were too preoccupied with your hairbrained plan."

Normally, a reminder of her own recklessness would have gotten her riled up, but he was right. Just like Alina and Sophia had been right. Yes, in the end, she'd figured out who killed Connor and Major. But it didn't bring Major back. *And* she hadn't been there when Aunt Maggie died. The only thing it had changed was that now she wouldn't be able to use her arm for several months.

"Sophia was right to call you. If I'd been thinking clearer, maybe I…" Gabi didn't finish the sentence. "I don't know what I would have done, so I'm glad she called. And, Agent Jacks, I'm grateful you listened. I don't even want to think about what would have happened if you hadn't been there."

"Well, when she spelled it all out for me, it was clear you were on to something. As I said, you'd make a great detective. And, Gabi, please, call me Bob."

20

———————

LATER THAN EVENING, Gabi sat on her couch, legs curled beneath her, staring off into space. With her free arm, she hugged the ridiculous Garden State Parkway Exit 137 sweat-shirt that her aunt had loved. The sounds of Sophia and Alina preparing something to eat drifted out from the kitchen. Probably one of the several oven-ready dishes that Alina had commandeered when they left their mother's.

Not ready to face her house alone, Gabi had planned to knock herself out the moment she got home, but both Alina and Sophia had insisted on spending the night. Sophia had actually been staying with her since she'd gotten back from the hospital, only leaving to feed Bugsy at the office and go home to change for the funeral.

Though it had only been five days, it felt like an eternity.

As Gabi mentally began cataloging the list of things she had to do to settle Aunt Maggie's affairs, the doorbell rang. With Sophia and Alina busy in the kitchen, she went to answer. It was yet another condolences delivery, this one from Harry & David.

Sophia and Alina came out from the kitchen as Gabi placed the delivery next to half a dozen others.

"Ooh, Harry & David," said Sophia.

"Who's it from?" asked Alina.

Gabi shrugged, too tired to deal with it.

"Can I open it?" asked Sophia. "I love Harry & David."

So did Gabi. In fact, her favorite chocolate mints were from Harry & David, a guilty pleasure both she and Major had discovered they shared. Just as that thought passed through her mind, Sophia opened the package to reveal five boxes of the dark chocolate mini-mints.

Alina opened the note that came with the chocolates, glanced at it briefly, and then handed it over to Gabi.

Words cannot express my gratitude for your help and my deepest condolences for your loss. I can never repay you for what you did for George. Know that you will always have a friend in me. – Violet

As tears streamed down her cheeks, Gabi couldn't help but laugh. Major had always thought he'd hidden his Harry & David chocolate mint vice from Violet. Clearly, he hadn't.

Sophia and Alina exchanged glances.

"What's so funny?" Alina asked.

Gabi looked at her best friend and her sister and smiled. She picked up a box of chocolates and pointed them at Alina. "What did Aunt Maggie always say?" she asked.

Alina looked confused, but for only a moment. "Life is short. Eat dessert first." Tears sparkled at the corner of her eyes.

"Exactly." Gabi grabbed a napkin from the cat-shaped holder that always sat on the table, opened the box, and dumped the chocolates out.

"*Pofta buna,*" she said, using the Romanian words for "good eating," a habit she'd picked up first from her dad and reinforced after years of living with Aunt Maggie.

Before she could take a bite, Sophia jumped up.

"Hold on a sec. We're missing one thing," she said and darted into the kitchen.

"What's she doing?" Alina asked.

"It's Sophia. Who knows."

A minute later, Sophia returned, a bottle of champagne in one hand and a bottle of peach juice in the other. "How about a bellini toast to Major and Aunt Maggie?"

"I'll grab glasses," Alina said.

Gabi watched Sophia and Alina mix up the bellinis, and though her heart ached—for Aunt Maggie, for Major, even for her dad—she couldn't help but smile.

Life is short, she thought to herself, *but with dessert, bubbly, and good friends, it's definitely not all bad.*

FIND AN ADVISOR

The best way to see the world is with the help of a professional travel advisor.

Need help finding one? Here are three resources that can help:

U.S.

ASTA Travel Advisor Directory— www.asta.org/traveler Services/advisor-directory

Canada

ACTA Travel Advisor Finder— https://bookwithatrave ladvisor.ca/find-your-professional-acta-travel-agent/

U.S. & Canada

Cruise Lines International Association's Travel Advisor Finder— https://cruising.org/en/find-a-travel-agent

ACKNOWLEDGMENTS

There are many people who helped me along my journey to bring this book to fruition, and I owe them all my deepest gratitude.

Thank you to my dad, the first person to read my earliest draft. Your encouragement helped me keep going, even years after I first started. Thank you also to my mom, whose belief in me and my desire to do it "right" helped me make some of the hard decisions.

Thank you to Matt Ragghianti for your excellent advice and belief that Gabi could be more believable and more likeable with a little bit more effort on my part. Thank you to my editor, Laura Apgar, whose editing skills took *Death of a Travel Advisor* to the next level.

Thanks also to my sensitivity readers, Diarmuid Ryan and Paloma Villaverde de Rico, for making sure I didn't unknowingly publish anything offensive. And to Dr. Michael Finkelstein, for answering my medical questions. Any medical-related errors in these pages are due to my playing with the facts.

Finally, thank you to Marius for always being there for me and having my back, even when you don't necessarily understand why.

ABOUT THE AUTHOR

Dori Saltzman has been writing about travel, both for consumers and the travel trade since 2007. She specializes in writing about cruising, as well as the business of selling travel for travel advisors. Her debut novel was inspired by her years of coverage of the cruise and travel agency industries (though she's never actually encountered a murder). When she's not writing – for work or pleasure – you can find her slowly ticking items off her travel bucket list, reading cozy mysteries, and hanging out with her clowder of rescue cats. She lives with her husband in NJ.